I0531536

Storylandia

The Wapshott Journal of Fiction

Issue 15

The Wapshott Press

Storylandia, Issue 15, The Wapshott Journal of Fiction, ISSN 1947-5349, ISBN 978-1-942007-01-2, is published at intervals by the Wapshott Press, PO Box 31513, Los Angeles, California, 90031-0513, telephone 323-201-7147. All correspondence can be sent The Wapshott Press, PO Box 31513, LA CA 90031-0513. Visit our website at www.WapshottPress.com This work is copyright © 2014 by Storylandia. The Wapshott Journal of Fiction, Los Angeles, California. All stories copyright © 2015 Julie Travis and are reprinted here with the copyright owner's permission. Copyright for the cover artwork is held by Julie Travis.

Storylandia is always seeking quality original short stories, novelettes, and novellas. Please have a look at our submission guidelines at www.Storylandia.WapshottPress.com or email the editor at editor@wapshottpress.com

Many thanks to William Akin for the proofread and editorial support.

Cover: "Highgate Cemetery, London, c1988" by Julie Travis. www.julietravis.wordpress.com

Storylandia

The Wapshott Journal of Fiction

Founded in 2009

Issue 15, Spring 2015

Edited by Ginger Mayerson

Table of Contents

Collected Stories
by Julie Travis

Collected Stories

by
Julie Travis

From the Bones

Of all of the wildness of Dartmoor, Fernworthy was probably his favourite part. The reservoir—an obvious man-made mark on the land—was balanced by the boggy forest that ran around one side of it and then, beyond that, the moorland with its two stone circles, adjacent to one another, open to the sky and the elements. The stone circles were also man-made but their age made that forgivable and they seemed as natural as the grasslands they stood in.

He had parted from his wife and daughter at the car park, leaving them to walk the relatively easy path around the reservoir while he had the prospect of slopping his way through the trees and out to the stones. The summer had so far been reasonably dry, so his booted feet only sank an inch or so into the mud, making his progress through the forest much quicker than he had anticipated.

And so to the stones. He had them to himself and spent a while in the southern circle, eyes shut, taking in the ambience before heading a few yards back towards the forest. It was only then that he took the metal detector from the bag slung across his shoulder. It was legal—probably—to search here, as long as he gave the area immediately around the circle a wide berth. He switched the metal detector on and began sweeping the area, in a circle around the circles.

When the detector bleeped, it was due north of the northern circle's centre. He grabbed the trowel from the bag and dug gently at the wet, peaty soil. He used the detector again, passing it over the small mound of dug soil and then over the hole, where it gave a pleasing, stronger bleep. He dug a little further and there, in the blackness of the soil, was a glimpse of that most precious metal, used for thousands of years to denote status and wealth: gold.

He dropped the metal detector and brushed soil away with his fingers to reveal thin threads of gold twisted over and over to form a solid torc, a neck ring, quite likely from prehistoric times. He reached down to claim the treasure and it was only when he grasped it that he realised that the coldness underneath was not vegetation but well-preserved flesh, and that the ancient jewellery still hung around an ancient throat.

As the prehistoric body was being carefully excavated by Devon archaeologists, two women looked down from the top of Rough Tor towards King Arthur's Hall. Unaware of the excitement in the neighbouring county, they focussed their binoculars on the strange rectangular site, named after the legend that King Arthur himself frequented the place, rather than evidence of its actual use, which was likely a Neolithic mortuary house. The site, often waterlogged after rain, had never been excavated, a fact that was not lost on either of the women.

"How long is it since you've been here?" asked Zoe.

"Years. Ten, maybe," said Vivienne. "It was after a dry summer then, too. A few of us managed to walk right across the site."

"And it spooked you?"

"In a good way. We definitely weren't alone there, but we weren't scared."

"Let's get there, then. I'm keen to see a Neolithic site that isn't circular."

They put their binoculars away and clambered down the rocky slope of the tor. Forty minutes of hard walking later, they came to the fence that surrounded King Arthur's Hall.

And there came the first surprise. Despite having had no more than drizzle in the last week, the Hall was almost completely under water. Large tussocks of grass poked out. They looked solid enough to stand on.

"I wasn't expecting it to be this wet," said Zoe, failing to hide her disappointment.

"It really shouldn't be," said Vivienne. "And we haven't walked all this way to look at the Hall from outside. Come on."

She opened the gate and they walked through, testing the ground with their sticks as they went. As they approached the Hall, still partly surrounded by its ancient stone fence, Zoe gasped.

"This place is amazing. It *feels* amazing. I'm not sure if it's good or bad."

Vivienne nodded. "I think we can get to the middle of the enclosure. Follow my path."

She tested the tussocks thoroughly before stepping onto them as they slowly made their way into the Hall. When she found a mound that was big enough for both of them, she beckoned Zoe to join her, then pointed her stick at the nearest corner.

"The stone slabs are lying over there. Nothing's been found anywhere else."

"That's because no one's looked," said Zoe and dipped her stick into the water. She was expecting some resistance and, finding none, stepped forwards to regain her balance. The edge of the tussock gave way and she was in the water. She had a moment of panic, imagining that she'd sink forever and never find the bottom, giving birth to a new legend about the place, until the temperature of the water hit her and she swore, soaked up to her knees.

"Shit! It's freezing."

Vivienne was already holding out her stick for the other woman to grab. "The walk back will warm you up. Now get out before the mud sucks your boots off."

After an ungainly struggle she made it back onto the tussock, swearing again as rain began sweeping across from Rough Tor. She was just about to berate her stupidity when she heard a sound, like a plug being pulled out of a bath. They both watched a huge bubble burst at the surface of the water, at the exact spot where Zoe had been standing moments before. It was followed by dozens of smaller bubbles. Then a dark hand appeared from the water and held itself aloft, silently demanding attention.

"Oh Zoe, what *have* you done?" murmured Vivienne. The ground rumbled beneath her as if in disquiet.

In Derriford Hospital, Professor Adam Caviler stood over the two bog-bodies. They had been brought to Plymouth for preliminary analysis and the first x-rays had been taken. Adam looked at the bodies again then returned to his study of the x-rays, hoping they would make more sense this time.

He had been expecting to have found a clear cause of death by now. Many bodies of this age, at first estimate around 2500–3000 years old, had suffered ritual deaths. A slit throat or a pierced skull was commonplace. But there was no such damage to the well-preserved flesh of either body, and the x-rays showed that both skulls, though flattened by the weight of time and the bog, were intact. Both victims, one male, one female, had old, healed fractures, but there was no evidence of violent death.

There were only the marks on the bones. Deep scratches covered every visible bone on the bodies. It was something he had never seen before.

Vivienne Vale had just arrived. For once, it was useful to have one of the finders present.

"Is the find in the press yet?" he asked her.

"Just sketchy reports, no real detail or mention of the torc. More of a novelty piece than anything of importance. Thanks so much for letting me come. I'm sure you've had loads of requests."

Adam smiled. "Only from every archaeologist in the West of England, as well as everyone back at Exeter." Then, with just a hint of condescension, he added, "But you should be here. You found him and you might be able to help. Would you like to see our two guests?"

Vivienne nodded enthusiastically and Adam carefully peeled back the wet cloth that covered the bodies. One was in a crouched position, standard burial practice for the era, but the other, the man found at King Arthur's Hall, had, as far as could be ascertained, lain flat like a modern burial.

"I've only just started my investigation, but there's no obvious cause of death, the bodies and skulls are intact. Of course, they could have been poisoned. We'll have to wait and see. But I want you to look at the x-rays. They've come up with something very unexpected. The bones are marked, as if they've been scratched or cut and I don't know how that's possible."

He handed her his iPad and Vivienne, butterflies of excitement in her stomach, saw the bones of the ancient dead. The body from Dartmoor still had the torc around her neck, in x-ray more like a slave's shackle than a display of high status. The body from Bodmin Moor had no such adornments. It seemed entirely ordinary—until she looked at the x-rays.

Every bone was marked.

"Could it be a disease of some kind?" she asked, at a loss for an explanation.

Adam shook his head. "No. Well, nothing that I'm remotely aware of."

"What about an animal? I've heard of raptors taking live lambs and marking the bones in the struggle."

"There are no wounds on the skin. What could have been big enough to cause that much damage?"

Vivienne enlarged a detail of the x-ray and peered at it.

"The marks are all different. Not like claws or talons. Could you possibly email these to me? I'd like to take some time over this."

"As long as you keep them to yourself. I'm going to do a few more x-rays, then I'll send you the lot."

Vivienne handed the iPad back and sat down on Adam's chair, with that familiarity he found so irritating. "Seems to me you need to take some of the flesh off to have a proper look. What about the bloke who found Fernworthy Woman? Has he been here?"

"No he hasn't, but he keeps ringing the University. He wants money for the gold torc find. Typical treasure hunter. As for chopping some skin off, I'll be removing a section of finger from each of them to do just that."

He motioned for Vivienne to vacate his chair and tried to make a joke of it. "Now leave me to my work or I'll call security."

Vivienne smiled and got up. "Perhaps these bones will change our knowledge of prehistory."

Professor Caviler said nothing and Vivienne closed the door quietly behind her as she left.

The email arrived two impatient days later. Vivienne printed off copies of the x-rays and studied the marks. They weren't haphazard, as she had seen before when bones showed evidence of attack, either by sword, axe, or animal, and they were of an even depth, shallow enough not to have greatly damaged either bog-body. In short, they weren't the cause of death, unless they were the results of a disease new to science. She compared the two bodies. The marks showed similarities but were far from identical. While it was almost certain that Fernworthy Woman lived and died during the Bronze Age, it was probable that King Arthur's Man dated from Neolithic times. How could two such similar cases date from such different periods in prehistory? If the venerated Professor Caviler was stumped, then how could she hope to find the answer?

She returned to Adam's email, then shut down the computer. The laptop, outdated before she'd even used it, took its time while she waited like she always did, not quite trusting the machine to turn itself off unless she was staring at it. At last it did and she was left with a black screen—momentarily.

In the screen's reflection appeared a shape; a human figure. Vivienne whirled around and, in what would later be to her shame, a light trickle left her bladder. The size and slender frame of the figure was that of a young girl, but the features were that of a monster. The naked figure was white, the whiteness of a creature that hides from daylight. The girl's skin had the texture of pastry; sagging in places, thin and almost torn in others. Her head, completely hairless, had a doughy appearance, the nose barely protruding, the face rounded with no allowance made for a pair of eyes. There was, at least, a mouth—a slit like a jab from a knife. Blind, she nevertheless stared at Vivienne.

"The answers you seek are in the landscape," she said. The words were slightly muffled. "Look to the landscape as well as to the bones. Let *John-of-the-Stars* guide you."

Was she dreaming? Vivienne felt like a child again, wanting to pull the blankets over her head after a nightmare, but unable to move.

The girl reached out towards her. Vivienne inched away.

"What do you want?" she whispered.

"I'm ravenous! I smell meat!" said the girl.

Vivienne backed away towards the fridge and took out the shoulder of lamb. It seemed heavier, more raw than when she'd bought it. She tore open the bag and gave the contents to the girl. In her plaster-white hands the meat looked like a hideous wound. The girl ripped the meat from the bone, opening her slit-mouth as far as it would go to push the food in quickly. She finished and held the bone up like a trophy. Then she dug her nails into it, carving marks around the surface. In the next instant she slipped down a gap in the floorboards and disappeared, and the bone dropped to the floor.

As she got out of her car at Fernworthy, Vivienne tried to fathom why she'd never visited the place before. The place was littered with rich archaeology—that alone should have made her a regular visitor.

After the nightmare girl had disappeared,

she spent two hours staring at the space the girl had inhabited. At times she stood in silence, at others she sat, drink in hand, whispering the things the girl had said, dreading her return. When everything remained as it was, as it should be, she had approached the bone that lay on the carpet, picked it up and inspected it.

The girl had made distinct marks with her long fingernails. Vivienne recalled the way the girl had gone about it—calmly, not in a frenzied attack. The marks were superficially similar to the ones on the skeletons of the bog people, as if the girl had been trying to show her what had been done and why. Was there a ritual element to the marks after all? Was the girl responsible for them, to have somehow been able to carve bone yet leave flesh and muscle intact?

But if that were so, the girl,—obviously a child despite her grotesque appearance—would be of incomprehensible age; three thousand or more years old.

It was only when Vivienne entered the forest that she realised why she'd never been before. She usually loved woodland but this was different. It had a grim air about it, the feeling that it was sucking her in, both physically and spiritually. She remembered then how uneasy she'd felt just looking at the forest on a map, thinking it was too dense to penetrate. It had seemed ridiculous at the time, but now she wondered if it had been a warning to be cautious.

After the rain of the last few days, the walk through the forest was hard going, her boots sinking deep into the mud at times but she took it slowly, determined not to panic. She had almost asked Zoe to accompany her but she couldn't explain how she had got her information. Zoe wouldn't have laughed at her description of the girl, she had an interest in mythology and ancient belief systems that gave her a more open mind than many, but Vivienne was incapable of speaking about what had happened. Not to Zoe and certainly not to Professor Caviler. For the Professor there was only evidence and fact. So Vivienne had undertaken the journey alone, and was beginning to regret it.

At last she was clear of the forest and she headed towards Fernworthy's double stone circle. The girl had said to look to the landscape. Had the finder of Fernworthy Woman missed something? Vivienne could see the stones now despite the rain. A man bobbed up into view. He seemed to be roughly in the place where Fernworthy Woman had been found. Perhaps it was the finder, digging around in the hope of unearthing more treasure.

But the man wasn't digging anything up. On the contrary; he was burying something.

John-of-the-Stars cursed at the heavy, wet soil. Every spadeful weighed twice as much as the one before. His back and neck were aching at the strain of the job so he stopped to rest. It was then that he spied the woman striding towards him. He ignored her and threw another load of earth into the hole. The woman came closer and tried to catch his eye but he simply cursed again and continued. This body was far too old for his needs. He would be grateful when it was over and he could return from where he came. The woman walked through the stones but was more interested in him than them. If she made trouble, he thought, he might just hit her with his spade and put her in the hole. Inevitably, she approached him.

"Hello. Are you using a metal detector?" she asked.

"I do not need a machine to detect metal," John-of-the-Stars replied. "It has a stink about it that makes it easy to find."

He sound irritated rather than concerned that whatever he was doing had been discovered. Vivienne took a gamble.

"My name's Vivienne. I'm an archaeologist. It's just that you need special permission to work here," she said, unsure of how true the assertion was. "Whether you're hunting for something or hiding something."

"So go tell a police officer," said John-of-the-Stars, shovelling the remaining mud into the hole.

Vivienne almost walked away, but the memory of the girl who had invaded her home willed her on. She couldn't leave without answers.

"Are you John-of-the-Stars? I've come about the bones. The marks on the bones, actually."

He stopped and gazed at her with a newfound interest.

"How do you know my name? No one knows my name."

Vivienne explained her involvement in the discovery of the bog bodies, the x-rays, and her bizarre visitor.

John-of-the-Stars scowled. "It was you! You spend your life *taking* from the Earth. You've learnt nothing and now you've damaged something more important than you can imagine. Humm should not have sent you here."

"Is Humm the girl? She said you'd help me. If I've done something wrong then tell me how I can right it. I've spent my life looking at the past, trying to learn from it. If I've transgressed something sacred then I'm truly sorry; it wasn't intentional."

John-of-the-Stars leant on his spade, easing his aching back. "Return the bodies to the Earth. Intact. Then pray the land forgives you."

He went back to work. The conversation was over. She made her way back towards the forest and the safety of her car. Once or twice she turned around, sure that someone was watching her, but there was no one to be seen.

Zoe parked in the lane near Vivienne's bungalow and knocked on the door. She usually loved coming here. The bungalow itself was shabby, comfortably so, and its position, just a couple of miles north of Tavistock, was isolated enough to be overwhelmed by the dome of stars that encompassed the place on clear nights. Tonight, however, she was feeling nervous. Vivienne had rung her and told her about Derriford and the stone circles. It was *vital*, she said, that they meet. It had sounded quite ominous.

Vivienne opened the door, a look of great relief on her face and all but dragged Zoe inside. She sat her down, poured each of them a drink and described in full the events of the last few days, holding a hand up for silence whenever Zoe tried to interrupt. When she'd returned to her car at Fernworthy she'd locked herself in and rung Professor Caviler, insisting that the bodies had to be returned, undamaged, to the moors for religious reasons. To her horror, he had dismissed the idea. Apart from the unorthodoxy of it, the request was impossible to carry out: samples had already been taken, part of a finger removed from each body, and the neck torc delivered to the British Museum.

"I hung up on him and drove home. I made a few calls and found out who discovered Fernworthy

Woman. It was a man from Lyme Regis, called Jason Ford. And he's gone missing."

Zoe stopped drinking. She needed a clear head to absorb everything Vivienne was telling her.

"Could there be another explanation for this girl you saw? Could something in the bodies have made you hallucinate?"

"If it had all happened at Derriford, then yes, I'd agree. But it didn't. And the Professor's seen nothing unusual. Oh, wait—I have proof! Wait here a minute."

She left the room and soon returned, laying the bone Humm had defaced on the coffee table.

"I've tried making those marks on another bone. A knife, a screwdriver, my own nails—nothing looks anything like them."

"And you think Jason Ford's disappearance is connected with this?" asked Zoe, running her fingers across the bone. "Do you really think we're in trouble because we found the bog-man?"

"I was being warned or threatened today. *And* yesterday, by the girl. The eminent Professor Caviler doesn't believe in anything that doesn't come with drawerfuls of evidence. I wasn't sure what I believed in, but the last couple of days have scared the shit out of me. I'm questioning everything."

"So it wouldn't hurt to be careful."

Vivienne nodded. "But most of all we need to work out what those marks on the bones are. That's what this is all about."

John-of-the-Stars was eating when Humm came calling. He hated to eat, as much as he hated to perform any bodily function. They were all things he'd left behind long ago, before he'd been dragged back to Earth to do his menial but essential work.

Humm appeared from one of the many cracks in the wall, squeezing her disgusting body into his home, then stood over him, sniffing at his food.

"My cairn's warmer than this hovel," she began, referring to her appropriated home in Fernworthy Forest, knowing that he considered her disrespectful for living in such a place.

"In my experience, deep space is warmer than this hovel," he said. "No matter. You went to the archaeologist's home and sent her to me. It was inconvenient and unnecessary."

"If the bodies are returned, then perhaps all will be well," said the girl. "It would be quicker, less blasphemous, that way."

John-of-the-Stars dropped his fork onto the plate and turned to face Humm. Her people had been around since before humans were human. *She* had seen several millennia come and go. That was deserving of respect, he reminded himself, and made his own existence seem trivial. But it was difficult not to be repulsed. Each time he saw her, the flesh had slipped a little further down her face. He turned away again before speaking.

"The bodies will undoubtedly be in pieces by now. And some of the work has already been restored. The archaeologist appeared just as I was finishing. She was blissfully ignorant, of course. It'll be easier to continue than to convince her to return the bodies."

He got up from the table. Before he was two paces away, Humm was working the remains of his dinner into her slit mouth.

They were both too jittery to be alone, so Zoe had slept in Vivienne's spare room. In the early morning, with the sun making a brief, blazing appearance before the rain came in again, the world seemed a surer place as they studied a set of x-rays each.

"Has an osteoarchaeologist seen these yet?" asked Zoe. "Or a zoo-archaeologist?"

"I don't know. The Professor's been in touch with the departments in Exeter and Bristol Universities, but I don't know what else has been going on. Depends on how territorial he's being."

Vivienne reached for a notepad and pen.

"Some of these markings seem to repeat. Do me a favour and copy as many of the markings from King Arthur's Man as you can."

They worked quickly. After half an hour, Vivienne looked up from the page.

"There's a pattern here, Zoe. It's not chaotic, like an attack or a disease would be."

Zoe was nodding. "Once I began writing them down, a couple of the marks reminded me of Runic or Ogham lettering. The shapes are quite beautiful."

They both fell silent.

Vivienne put her pen gently on the table. The significance of what Zoe had said, and of what she suspected, was huge.

It wasn't an osteoarchaeologist they needed, but an ancient languages expert.

The marks on the bones were script.

And in the rain, pouring down, too, on Bodmin Moor, a sigh could be heard, if anyone had been there to hear it, on Rough Tor, as the rock strewn ground rose, settled and rose again. Disquiet was taking shape.

Zoe had to go to work, so Vivienne packed up the x-ray printouts and notepads and drove them both to Plymouth. She dropped Zoe off and headed to

Derriford Hospital. Professor Caviler was in the cafeteria having breakfast. Vivienne hadn't dared ring him; the theory she and Zoe had come up with needed to be explained face to face. She bought them both coffee and apologised for the strange phone call she'd made from Fernworthy.

"I haven't had time to test the theory extensively, but from the work we did this morning, I'd estimate there could be a hundred or more separate types of marks, repeated all over the two bog-bodies. The marks are repeated too often, too accurately, to be coincidental. I'd really like someone more qualified to have a look."

She didn't tell him about Humm or John-of-the-Stars. She needed him onside—one word about either of them would have put him at his most dismissive. She handed over the pages she and Zoe had worked on.

"I don't know," said Adam, frowning and shaking his head. "The way you've written them down makes the marks *look* ordered. Are you finding real patterns here? Or are you creating them to make sense of the marks?"

"I don't think so, but I'm not sure. That's why I think a language expert should study the x-rays." said Vivienne.

Adam dropped the sheet he was holding. "This is absurd. If the bodies were skeletons I could accept the theory as worth pursuing. But the bodies are in virtually perfect condition. Were they born with writing on their bones? Did they go about their daily lives like that? Of course not. There's another explanation."

He excused himself and got up from the table, bought another coffee, and went back to the X-Ray

Department and his makeshift laboratory. The bog-bodies were being moved to Exeter University soon, much to his relief. It would be easier to work on them in the familiar, well-equipped lab there, and he would not be making the time-wasting commute to Plymouth. As for Vivienne's bizarre theory, Bristol University's osteo-archaeologist, who had been analysing the two sections of finger, would soon arrive and blow it out of the water. There would be order, certainty, the ability to give sensible answers to sensible questions. He let himself in to the lab and switched on the light.

Only to find the fragile, white figure of Humm crawling elatedly over Fernworthy Woman.

Disorder reigned supreme.

Humm had left John-of-the-Stars' hovel at Manaton and travelled southwest across Dartmoor, sliding down streams and rivers wherever possible, ducking behind boulders when the fresh air made her anxious, making her way to Plymouth. Derriford Hospital was located to the north of the city and, once in the outskirts, Humm had crawled down into the drains. She slithered along the sewerage system, eating any unfortunate rats that came her way, and followed a pair of huge cockroaches into Derriford's morgue. With their peaty smell, the bog-bodies had been easy to locate in the vast hospital building, and Humm had been greeting them when Adam had walked in. Had she not felt the section of finger missing from each one and the tissue samples taken from the bodies, Humm would happily have returned them to their original resting places, but John-of-the-Stars had been right; the bodies had been violated. Humm was horrified. She leapt onto the Professor, tore out clumps of his hair and spat furious, muffled words in his face.

"These chapters have been defiled! Pieces are missing! Where are they?"

Adam struggled for breath, far too close to that big, eyeless face for comfort.

"They've... been sent... for analysis," he grunted.

Humm jammed her fist into Adam's mouth to silence him.

"Then the text must be rewritten," she said.

She wrapped him up in a bedsheet, so tightly he could barely move, then heaved herself and the bundle out of a window, into a quiet part of the hospital grounds. Once outside the confines of the building, she began to run. At first she carried the bedsheet over one shoulder like a sack. She made no attempt to hide as she had on her way in to the city; people stared or screamed as she sprinted past them. Once she'd left the streets behind, crossed two fields and found the beginnings of the moor, Humm began to relax. She lowered the bedsheet and dragged it alongside her as she ran, ignoring Adam's screams as he bounced over rocks and gorse and splashed through streams.

The ordeal seemed to last for hours. Several times he was knocked unconscious then awoken by a soaking from a stream to find the nightmare wasn't over. Near the top of Alex Tor, out of sight of the road, Humm stopped to rest. The rain had begun again. Steam rose from her body. She sat on a boulder and let the bedsheet go. Adam, bloodied and bruised, had a glorious view of daylight then, as the sheet fell away, a profile of Humm, gasping and catching her breath.

"Vivienne's been having strange ideas," he whined to himself. "Now I'm hallucinating. The bog-bodies must be toxic."

Hearing him, Humm looked down. "Bog-bodies? They were people—royal people—who served a great purpose. Until they were stolen."

"On the contrary," said Adam, his wits more about him now. Hallucination or not, he was not going to lose an argument. "Finding them should teach us a great deal about the past. The bodies might end up in a museum. They'll be treasured and taken great care of."

"Great care was being taken of them where they were. Now two graves lie empty, or rather, one grave remains so; John-of-the-Stars has filled the other."

Adam looked at his captor in disgust. The repulsive girl was clearly a lunatic. She had the strength of several men and was able to find her way around despite having thick flesh where her eyes should be. He recalled the way she had been slavering over a corpse. She was as pitiful as she was frightening. But some of what she was saying sounded close to the rubbish Vivienne had been hinting at. Had the girl managed to influence Vivienne?

Humm ranted for a while, about sacred writings and defilement, then twisted around and down so that her face was close to Adam's.

"Do you feel the ground beneath you?" she hissed. "You feel the cold and the wet, but go deeper. Be still and you'll feel the ground moving, growing. If you're lucky, you might feel its heart beat. It lives and breathes and is not to be ransacked whenever it takes your fancy to do so."

Humm's breath was vile. Adam shrank back into the bedsheet but Humm whipped it away.

"I'm tired! You will take us the rest of the way. You'll contact the woman who took from the Cornish moor. She must meet us at the circles outside Fernworthy Forest. John-of-the-Stars will be there and the land will be restored."

Humm dragged Adam upright. With shaking hands he felt for his mobile phone and to his relief found he had a signal. As he dialled Vivienne's number his cold, fleshy captor climbed upon his back and wrapped her limbs around him, squeezing his ribs just hard enough to show she could crush his bones if she wished.

"Now *run!*" she shrieked.

And so it was that Vivienne returned to her car in Plymouth and took a call from a man who was no longer sure of his place in the world. Vivienne agreed to the meeting immediately. She stopped briefly at the café where Zoe worked and claimed a family emergency for dragging her away. Despite Zoe's protestations, Vivienne dropped her off at her bungalow.

"You can drive home if you want," she said. "Although you could work on the markings here. You're *not* coming with me; I've got no idea what's going to happen. I'll contact you as soon as I can. Lock the door."

She wanted to get to Fernworthy quickly, so drove north to the trunk road, across the top of Dartmoor and south to Chagford before hurtling down the narrow lanes to the forest car park. The rain had persisted for days now and the mud covered her shoes and leaked through to her socks in minutes. Still she hurried as best she could, shivering as the forest enclosed her again. Several times she almost fell but managed to cling to a branch. At last she cleared the forest and headed through the boggy ground to the circles.

Inside the southern circle, sat with his back against a stone that gave some protection against the rain, was John-of-the-Stars. He barely looked at her as she plodded between the stones.

"The thief returns," he said.

She almost corrected him—it had, after all, been Zoe who had dislodged the body at King Arthur's Hall—but if Zoe had been forgotten about, then so much the better. So instead, she asked where the Professor and Humm were.

"They are coming across country, so they may be some time," he said.

She settled down as best she could, grateful for a little shelter.

John-of-the-Stars closed his eyes. "Know that this is the meeting point for many things today," he said, in such a way that Vivienne wasn't sure who he was addressing. "Things that may take the form of miracles or nightmares, depending on your point of view," he continued. He cocked his head to one side, hearing something despite the wind. Then he turned around and squinted southwestward, into the rain.

A sound was being carried on the wind. To Vivienne it *was* the wind, making its way across the moor, but John-of-the-Stars grabbed the stone he'd been leaning against and hauled himself up. Vivienne did likewise and peered through the rain.

A strange shape was approaching them at speed.

It came down the hill and reached the bottom, disappearing for a moment as it crossed a dip, then appearing once again.

It looked human but *different.*

It was too tall, too oddly shaped. And it made a terrible sound, a scream of distress and joy from its two gaping mouths as it sped towards them.

The shape became clearer. It was Professor Caviler, running faster than any human should be able to run, with Humm upon his back. Both were screaming, had been screaming for some time judging by the hoarseness of their voices. Adam ran through bogs that came up to his expensively-trousered thighs, leapt boulders that were half his height, all the time urged on by Humm, who dug her fat, white heels into his ribcage and waved a hand so quickly that it cracked like a whip. The Professor's features, more distinguishable by the minute, were an agony of exhaustion. He looked as if he might drop down dead before he reached the stone circle. He stumbled at the last moment, sprawling into the mud between two of the stones and throwing Humm to the centre of the circle. Humm recovered quickly but Adam lay where he fell, his wet hair stuck across his face and merging with his beard.

Humm wiped the drizzle from her head and shook some of the water from her body. The rain was easing. There was no sign of anyone else on the moor. Vivienne did not expect there to be. No one was going to intervene in whatever was about to happen.

"Do you know why the humpback whale's song changes each time it is sung?" asked Humm. She had produced the hospital bedsheet and wrapped it around her like a cloak. It was splattered with mud, blood and dirty water.

"It does not change greatly," she continued, explaining not only to Vivienne, Adam, and John-of-the-Stars but to the standing stones, the forest and the earth beneath her feet. "And all humpbacks sing the same song. But year by year it is altered. And the reason for this is that the humpback is telling the younger whales their story, their history, adding to it over time. In this way the whales record and spread their great knowledge of the past. Such wisdom! All life needs such things—records and documents and stories." She pointed towards Vivienne. "Humans have done this in different ways for many thousands of years. And so has the land."

She stopped suddenly; staring, somehow, at Vivienne.

"You mean in its geology, or the rings inside tree trunks?" said Vivienne, who felt obliged to offer something. "When we first met you said to look to the landscape. Is that what you meant?"

"The rocks and trees and peat will tell *you* some things," said Humm, "but the Earth needs to record its own history for its own purposes."

Vivienne glanced down at Adam, hoping he was able to take this in, but there was only bafflement on his face. Vivienne suddenly wished Zoe were there to see herself proved right.

"So the carvings on the bones are writing?" said Vivienne. "I don't see how that's possible. Who carved them? And how? If we'd found skeletons, I might understand."

"You are nowhere near close to understanding," hissed Humm. "You shall meet the author of the text."

Vivienne looked around but could see no one.

"Behold!" said Humm, gesturing towards an anonymous-looking piece of moorland not far from the stone circles.

The ground began to rise. It pulled grass and bog up with it and became a small hill. Vivienne grabbed one of the stones. It held firm. Had something been lying underneath the moor all this time, some angry creature waiting to reveal itself? She waited for the hill to burst open but instead it began to take shape. Two arms of mud and grass wrenched themselves free and raised themselves above the hill that was now forming a head and the top half of a torso. The arms grew hands and fingers. They heaved at the ground to liberate the rest of the body. Four wet, peaty legs were pulled from the soil and the creature—*of* the land, not hiding within it—stood upright, towering over them all.

John-of-the-Stars glanced up but chose not to meet the scrutiny of its one central eye. Vivienne felt her bladder spasm. Determined not to lose control of it this time, she clenched every muscle in her body. Only Humm seemed at ease, excited at the land-beast's appearance. She paced around the stone circle before leaping onto Professor Caviler again.

"Where in Hell did *that* come from?" he asked, through teeth that chattered so hard they sounded about to break.

"You've learnt nothing! Nothing!" said Humm. "He is not separate from the Earth, he *is* the Earth. And today he shall be known as *The Flight of Swallows.*"

The Flight of Swallows bent over the stone circle to address them.

"I am the Earth, the sky, the air, the sea," he said in a voice that was like the beating of a hundred thousand pairs of wings. "I am a tiny part of everything alive and dead. The land has its own language, its own story. We have documented this story for millions of years."

"You took part of the text." said Humm, pointing at Vivienne before turning on Adam. "And you desecrated it."

"A body has been returned to the soil here," said The Flight of Swallows. "Another must be returned to the Cornish moor. And the missing chapters must be rewritten, here and now."

Vivienne managed to tear her gaze from The

Flight of Swallows and looked across to John-of-the-Stars, remembering him digging the soil outside the stone circle.

She knew he had been burying something. And now she had a sickening idea of what it was.

"Did you bury Jason Ford over there?" she asked.

"I believe that was his name," said John-of-the-Stars. "He died quietly, just before he went into the ground. He understood the enormity of what he had done."

Vivienne was sure she would not die quietly.

"I'll get the bodies back from the hospital, I promise," she said. "I'll put them back, exactly as they were." She was willing to do anything to pacify the miraculous nightmare that stood over her.

But all she did was agitate him. A huge hand swiped past her in annoyance and knocked one of the standing stones out of the ground.

Adam thought of the two sections of finger he'd removed and sent to Bristol University, of Humm clasping the damaged hands. Returning the bog-bodies would not be enough. A sacrificial lamb was required.

"I took those bodies in good faith," he appealed to The Flight of Swallows. "Vivienne took the Cornish man from the ground. This is all down to her." He shuddered as water and grass rained down from above.

"As I understand it," said John-of-the-Stars, "Vivienne was not the one who unearthed the man at King Arthur's Hall. Save your pitiful attempts at blame. No one here is going to die today."

The Flight of Swallows crouched down and spoke to them all. "The text must first be carried amongst the living. The story of the land will resonate from your bones."

Professor Adam Caviler was first.

The Flight of Swallows' technique of defleshing without causing pain or damage was a sight to behold. Vivienne watched as Adam's skin was peeled away from his skull from a single, neat cut to the top of his head, his bones bared without shame. Adam did not scream or flinch. Indeed, he seemed to be far away from what was happening.

Once his skeleton had been revealed The Flight of Swallows pulled something from his own muddy flesh. It looked like flint; dark, chipped to a fine point like a Stone Age tool. The Flight of Swallows set to writing. He steadied Adam's body with one hand and, with the greatest skill, began carving script onto every inch of the bones, each mark a word or phrase as beautiful and powerful as Life itself. When he was finished, he dressed Adam back in his skin. When he was sure every piece of flesh was in its right place, he gave Adam to John-of-the-Stars to re-clothe and take care of.

Then it was Vivienne's turn.

She felt a spike of pain at the top of her head, then numbness. She watched her skin peeled away to rest on the cold, wet ground, then The Flight of Swallows was holding her, gently, so as not to damage her. She looked up into his eye. It shimmered like water, the iris the colour of sunset. It seemed to her to hold no malice.

She heard him carving the ancient script onto her spine, along her ribs, over her skull. She saw the bones of her arms and legs decorated with the story of the planet and as The Flight of Swallows wrote she saw the extract of the amazing tale flash before her lidless eyes; huge, multi-finned creatures roaming the seas, living, dying, eventually becoming extinct, the planet itself evolving, a Thing as alive and glorious as any creature that had ever stood upon it.

When it was done she felt something close to sorrow.

Humm dressed her once her skin had been returned. Her tone had changed; it was now almost reverential.

"You will live a long and joyful life. And when you die I will come for you and bury you in a sacred place. The missing chapters will have been replaced. All will be well."

She was helped to her feet and stood at Adam's side. The Flight of Swallows instructed them.

"For now we shall all return to our lives. Humm is the curator of the bones and you will see her in your dreams or your waking lives, from time to time. John-of-the-Stars has one more task, to replace the missing corpse on the Cornish moor. Then his work is done and back to the stars he shall go. Treat your bodies well," he clasped Vivienne and Adam by the shoulder, "and may your bones stay strong."

Adam, wild-eyed but silent, began to walk, taking lurching steps like a drunk. Vivienne turned to see The Flight of Swallows one more time. He was smaller, his body losing definition as he sank back to the boggy mud.

John-of-the-Stars stepped forward and spoke to her.

"Don't hurry home. Your friend, the desecrator of graves, is there. Better that I've been and gone before you get back."

The text was heavy on her bones, her skin

tingling as feeling returned. It was like learning to walk again. Vivienne knew she was too slow, too clumsy, to be able to save Zoe, and the knowledge hurt. Her grief added to the weight of the responsibility she carried.

She took Adam's hand to calm him and, step by staggering step, they made their way back across the moor, towards Fernworthy Forest.

Grave Goods

His father had told him, "You can't take it with you when you go."

This pearl of wisdom usually came halfway through a bottle of single malt. *The good stuff; none of that blended rubbish.* The way he spent money made Eddy Dobbs think his father could die at any moment. Did his father know something he didn't? As he got older Eddy realised his father, like everyone else, expected to live forever. It was just a saying to excuse his rampant selfishness. Eddy and his mother went without while his father did his best to have nothing left in this world, never mind the next. All he came home with at the end of the day were brutish words for his mother (as damaging as the occasions when he'd beat her with his fists) and resentment for his son, usually referred to as *the waste of space* or *the little poof*. And when he did let his fists do the talking, Eddie tried to protect his mother, but he was brushed aside. A child cannot keep a monster at bay. But Eddy worried that he'd *let* himself be pushed away, because he was frightened, of his father, of being hurt. He hated his fear almost as much as he hated his father. When the man died, he was buried wearing his gold sovereign ring and chunky gold bracelet. Aged just twelve, Eddy nevertheless realised this was one last act of selfishness: if the bastard really couldn't take it with him then no one else was going to have it either. While what little the jewellery was worth lay underground, unclaimable and of no use to anyone, Edward Dobbs Senior would appear in the Afterlife, bereft of his ring and bracelet but laughing at the fact that his family had nothing but bitter times and debts to remember him by.

Like father, like son. That was another saying which chilled him to the bone when he heard it and never failed to wind him up. There were traces of his father in him—the shrug of the shoulders when a stranger was in trouble (although his father would have shrugged if his own family were screaming for help), the selfishness that reared up every now and then and had to be tempered. He hated those parts of his nature and fought them all his life, looking to his mother's ways for guidance. She had tried to compensate for her husband, veering into martyrdom at times, but she always had time for anyone and anything. More than once she'd rescued a bird from the neighbour's cat and nursed it back to health.

Now fifty two years into his life, Eddy had achieved more than his father could have contemplated doing, and more than enough to make his mother proud. He had married Rachel thirty years ago and though there had been no children, it had not been an issue between them. On the contrary, it had given them a freedom other couples envied. Of late, however, things had been drifting and Eddy was determined to get the relationship back on course. On this day he had left work early and was browsing in the more interesting shops of the London suburb where he lived. The pawnbrokers, the charity shops, a tale of death or hardship behind most of the items for sale. He was looking for something for his wife, to try to break the ice that was forming around them.

Nothing poncey, and nothing tacky either. Something intriguing or humourous.

He found it in one of the charity shops. His eyes had been drawn to a gold sovereign ring. It was the first one he'd seen in years and he had a wild thought that it was his father's, that Edward had resurrected himself purely to piss the value of the ring up the wall or blow it on the horses. He even imagined he could see specks of earth on it, the result of Edward clawing his way out of his supposed resting place. But this was a charity shop and people gave things to charity shops. It couldn't possibly be his father's.

Next to it was another ring. It was old, silver, and had some class. It had the head of a cat on it, but it wasn't something for a child—it was artistic and finely crafted. The tag on the ring simply said, 'Victorian Mourning Ring. £30'. He asked the woman at the counter if she knew anything about it.

"Unusual, isn't it?" she said. "The Victorians often had mourning rings made, but for dead family members. I didn't know they did them for pets."

"More money than sense, eh?" said Eddy. "Still, it's very interesting. I'll take it."

He hoped it would fit one of Rachel's fingers, otherwise the gift could turn out to be more of an insult than a bridge-builder.

As it turned out, the ring only fitted her left thumb. Eddy was about to remark that *only queers wear rings on their thumbs, don't they?* but Rachel was so delighted he kept quiet, pleased at her reaction. It was a good feeling.

The good feeling continued to the weekend when, instead of their usual separate ventures, Rachel suggested they have lunch together. At her suggestion, they went to his favourite place. Kate's

Kitchen in Notting Hill had survived and defied the gentrification that had the rest of the area in its grip. It was a straightforward café serving good, straightforward food. He went to the counter and ordered all-day breakfasts and coffee, paid, and even had the good humour to chat to the lad behind the counter. He returned to his table and was brought up short.

There was someone sitting with Rachel. From the back the person looked clearly male—all slicked back hair, shirt, and braces. But when he got to his chair he found he really wasn't sure of the stranger's gender. The person was thin, had neither facial hair nor make-up, and appeared to be wearing jodhpurs, like some old fashioned toff. Rachel evidently knew him or her, judging by the way the pair were chatting.

"Oh Eddy, I'm glad you're back. This is a friend of mine, Marlowe."

"Hello, Eddy," said Marlowe. "I've heard a lot about you."

The voice was too high to be male but too low to be female. A hand was proffered. Eddy shook it. It was tiny but matched his easily in strength. Eddy managed to make conversation until Marlowe looked at the clock on the wall and said *it* had to go. Breakfast arrived and Eddy waited until they were tucking in before asking a few questions.

"I've never heard you mention a Marlowe. No offence, but I couldn't tell if they were male or female. Seemed nice, though."

Rachel smiled. "She *is* a bit eccentric, isn't she? Looks like a gentleman, acts like one, too, but she's a little Cockney sparrow underneath, you mark my words. I've known her for a while. Can't remember how we met."

A mannish woman was easier to be seen with than an effeminate man, although a gay man was better, safer, as a friend for his wife, Eddy thought.

"Yeah, well, as long as she knows you're spoken for," he said, smiling as much as he could.

Rachel laughed. "She hasn't tried any funny business, if that's what you're worried about. She was just admiring my new ring, actually. Said it was very evocative."

It was time to rein it in, Eddy thought. No point in having a row over some weirdo. They continued their meal in contented silence.

The whole weekend went well. There was an air about them both, of hope, perhaps, that things could get much better if they made an effort. Eddy started the working week with a bit of a spring in his step. The market stall, where he'd grafted since he was sixteen and now ran, was a tough business to make money from, but he loved it. The buzz of the crowds, the community of traders, the damn heritage of the place: Portobello Road was legend and he was part of it. His banter was ever more humourous and risqué as the day went on and everyone was enjoying it. He was loading empty crates into his van at the end of the afternoon when a late punter stepped into view. With the sun behind them, the person was silhouetted at first, but when Eddy squinted, he could see properly. To his annoyance, he realised it was Marlowe. Crouched inside the van, he felt trapped.

"Mr Dobbs. Sorry to bother you at work but I wondered if I might have a word."

He– she, Eddy reminded himself, was polite enough. Eddy decided to give her a break; be unselfish.

"Hello, Marlowe. What brings you here? You're a bit late for the market, I'm afraid."

"I know, Mr Dobbs. It was you I came to see."

This was not a coincidence, then. Eddy felt a cloud appear on his horizon.

"We need to have a talk," Marlowe continued. "In private. It's of the utmost importance, I assure you."

Eddy drove them to a quiet side street. A few people were around but that didn't matter. This was London—people minded their own business and no one gave them a second glance.

"Is this about Rachel?" said Eddy. He half expected Marlowe to challenge him to a duel over her.

"It is not," said Marlowe. "Despite your insecurity, I'm not interested in your wife and I wouldn't ask your permission if I was. I got to know her because I was looking for you. I should tell you what I do. I'm an Intermediary. I negotiate between parties in the Otherworld and the Land of the Living."

Eddy tried to suppress a guffaw but couldn't. Eccentric didn't cover it. The woman was a nutter.

"Your father wants your forgiveness. And his ring, if you please."

Eddy stopped laughing.

"The mourning ring that you brought Rachel was mine. It has the strength to mend a broken heart. Rachel will need it."

Eddy grabbed Marlowe by her collar. "You come out with this bullshit! You've been fishing for information on me from my wife. What for? What kind of scam are you working?"

Marlowe just looked at him. She wasn't frightened. It was weird. Eddy let her go. Mad or not, scammer or not, he was not going to punch a woman.

"I have good and bad news for you, Mr Dobbs. Your father did leave you an inheritance after all; a predisposition for liver cancer. It killed him and shortly it will kill you. The good news is that your father was wrong."

It was time to get her out of the van and go home. She could witter away on the pavement.

"You *can* take it with you when you go," she said. "You *can* take things to the Otherworld."

She got out when he yanked the door open after almost running around the van from his side. Despite himself, he spat on the ground next to her.

Like father, like son.

Ten days later Eddy collapsed. He woke up in hospital to the news that his body was, frankly, screwed. He was riddled with cancer. There was a massive tumour in his liver that had spread to his major organs and elsewhere, everywhere else, it seemed. There was no saving him. He had a month or so left of staggering along and then a rapid decline and death.

Rachel was there to hear the stunning news and they wept over each other when the doctor had gone. But mostly Eddy was angry, seething. The things he still wanted to do, the marriage that, with a bit of work, could still last for decades. Time for retirement, a bit of travel, some happy, lazy times. He'd earned it.

He saved the anger for when Rachel had gone home for the night, then he shuffled to the toilet and punched the wall until his knuckles bled. It helped him to think straight. There were things to do, finances to sort out so that Rachel was as comfortable as possible after he'd gone. It was about being unselfish.

That made him think of his father, which in turn made him think of Marlowe. How could she possibly have known he was ill? He needed to talk to her. He left the cubicle, still dabbing his knuckles with toilet paper and there she was. Standing at the urinal, facing it as if she were pissing.

"How are you feeling, Mr Dobbs?" she said. "You've had a difficult day."

"I'll live," said Eddy. "For now, anyway. You've got some explaining to do. How did you find out?"

She was still facing the wall. "Your father told me. He only found out what killed him after he died."

"Drinking killed him, end of story," said Eddy. "But let's get back to me. I want to know how you knew." Then something appalling occurred to him and he grabbed Marlowe's shoulder and turned her to face him.

"Did you do this to me? Did you poison me?"

Marlowe removed his hand from her shoulder. "Of course not. Why would I? The tests you've had are quite conclusive. You have cancer. It is a tragedy but it's nobody's fault."

Eddy went to the sink and ran cold water over his bloody hand. It was intensely painful but unbelievably good.

"However," Marlowe continued, "you have a chance that not many people get. You have a little time before you are incapacitated. You have the opportunity to take whatever you want to the Otherworld. You have the chance to meet with your father and let him make amends. I can help you."

There was silence for a while. Eddy was tired. He just wanted Marlowe to go away. It was she who spoke first.

"I understand that you won't believe me at this stage. But think about it. You can take something precious; a lot of bartering is done there. Or take something to remind you of life here, your status in the Land of the Living, if that's what you want.

Anything at all."

"My father was an absolute bastard," Eddy finally replied. "Why would you think I'd want to see him again? Hypothetically speaking."

"Of course. People who are offered *grave goods* take all kinds of things for all kinds of reasons. Including the means to take revenge on someone or something that has wronged them in Life. I've met your father. I'm well aware of his shortcomings. I'm an Intermediary, not a diplomat. I take messages back and forth, I don't broker peace. That's up to you."

And she left him to his thoughts.

Six weeks went by. Eddy was discharged and, fired up to make the most of what time was left, set about tidying his affairs as best he could. He sold his business, made sure his Will was up to date and, most importantly, spent time with Rachel. The spring weather was cold but they spent hours just sitting in the garden together, wrapped up and sipping hot drinks. They were times to treasure.

He had planned to take his own life when things got too much, but the chance didn't come. He'd had an extra couple of weeks of useable time and he was grateful, but his health deteriorated so suddenly he was too weak for suicide and besides, the remaining moments were precious. It was only when it came to his final night that he thought of Marlowe and, just to pass the time while Rachel, perched on the bed beside him, was sleeping, he tried to think of what he'd take with him if he could.

Photos. A stack of them, friends and family. Mother, anyway.

Letters from Rachel from when they were courting.

The cap Old Len from the market had given him. Len, long dead, had been a market stalwart. Eddy would proudly wear it in the Otherworld (hypothetically, of course).

But if he *was* able to meet his father again, what else would he need? Marlowe had talked of revenge. What she'd said about his illness, his premature death, was bullshit. Of course it was someone's fault. Despite, or perhaps because of, the meds, the pain and his sheer *pissedoffness* at having everything taken away from him by his father, Eddy fantasised about getting his own back. For him and his mother, bless her departed soul. If Edward Senior wanted forgiveness, it was so he could get something out of it. If he wanted his tacky sovereign ring, Eddy might just take it to him and shove it down his whining throat.

He remembered how, some years ago, he had typed something perfectly innocent into a search engine and had been presented with terrible images and descriptions of Medieval torture. Cruelty had been an art form to these people. Images came back to him now; rats made to eat their way through human stomachs, tools designed to crack bones or peel flesh away, heavy iron face masks with deep plates attached to the top to pile hot coals upon.

Eddy laughed, although whether in his head or out loud he didn't know. Rachel slept on. He watched her for a moment. He realised that he wanted Marlowe to be telling the truth. He wanted to make his father pay.

"I need ta speak... to th'Innermediary," he mumbled.

No sooner said than done; Marlowe was at his side.

"Why would you do this for me?" Eddy asked.

"All I've done is bring you a message and made

you aware of your options."

"I want to take a photo of me and Rachel. On our wedding day."

Marlowe nodded. "That's easy enough. Rachel can put one in the pocket of whatever you're being buried in. You *do* need to be buried, not cremated. Is that a problem?"

With difficulty, he thought about it. Yes. He had a plot in the cemetery. A double plot, for them both, all paid for.

"It's okay. I'm being buried. I want some weapons. Not a gun. Something with a bit more…"

"Suffering?" suggested Marlowe. She thought for a moment. "There are instruments, *Damnation Irons*, that might be what you're after. They're ancient. They will wring pain from a soul for aeons. And they're beautifully crafted. But I warn you, they're cruel."

She took her phone out and showed him some photographs. The small screen couldn't contain the hideous intentions of the implements. The photos showed them at rest, displayed on plain linen sheets. A neckband with vicious looking spikes, able to slowly screw inwards at the turn of a small handle. A hand shaped cage that could slowly stretch and pull a hand to pieces. A heavy box to house genitalia and who knew what else. They had been well kept and were, as Marlowe said, the result of hours of highly skilled labour. In Hell, presumably.

"If you're really sure you want these, I will see they're in your coffin before the funeral. So no open casket. I have your father's ring. I will attach it to one of the Damnation Irons if you wish. It can help them work better. And he did want it back. Then I shall arrange a meeting between you and your father in the Otherworld."

Eddy wanted to giggle. At last! Revenge! It was an insane conversation, undoubtedly a combination of his imagination and medication. Hooray for opiates.

"Are you dead?" he asked.

"Don't be ridiculous!" Marlowe snorted.

"Why didn't my father take his shitty jewellery with him? He was buried wearing it."

"That's as far as it went. He wasn't offered the option of taking grave goods. I suppose it could be seen as breaking the rules for you to take his ring, but no one could blame your intentions."

"He can admire it on his finger til it's pulled apart," Eddy said, and sniggered. Then, in a moment of clarity, he whispered, "You *will* keep an eye on Rachel, won't you? I've provided for her financially but she'll need a friend."

Marlowe looked down at him. "I shall be there for her, Mr Dobbs. You have my word."

When Rachel woke up, she found Eddy had died. He was facing her, a look of deep contentment on his face.

Eddy's funeral was a quiet affair. He had no family to mourn him except his wife and her strange friend. Some of his market trader friends appeared, almost silent at the service but happy to drink and make amusing banter at the wake. They assumed it was expected of them.

It was in the chapel of rest, before the funeral, where the real activity of the day occurred. Marlowe, in her best black suit, had gained access without difficulty, although the case containing the Damnation Irons was heavy and had taken some time to pull through the window she'd opened. Once inside, she set the case down and got to work. She unscrewed the coffin lid. Eddy had been arranged to look as if he were sleeping but, like any corpse, the overriding effect was the absence of life. Marlowe wasn't fooled. The soul lurked, awaiting entrance to the Otherworld, and Eddy's soul was more anxious than most. Happy that his body was wearing a good suit, Eddy's soul wanted to see what the Damnation Irons looked like and how Marlowe would arrange them in the coffin, but this, apparently, was not allowed. Marlowe had told Eddy that the arrangement was secret, but it was very important that the soul appeared in the Otherworld in the form that the body was buried in (if it were human. Marlowe had wittered on about how it was for birds and plants and animals but Eddy, bored by then, had not been listening), and that there was a ritual about the placing of the Damnation Irons, more so than for any other grave goods, since they needed to be ready to use.

Marlowe undid the case and opened it up. It had been made specifically for the contents, which were several centuries old but in pristine condition. They smelt strange, a mixture of ancient iron and oil, and the ingredients used to charge them and increase their effectiveness: the blood of a rare bird, a bright orange fungus that grew on moorland trees, the skin of a snake. It took some time to arrange them correctly, and Marlowe was a perfectionist, but when it was done she screwed the lid back on the coffin, took the empty case. and climbed up to the open window.

"There you are, Mr Dobbs. Just as you requested," she whispered as she slipped away.

At the graveside Rachel grasped the beautiful mourning ring and silently blessed Marlowe for her strength. The woman's arm was tight around her, keeping her upright whenever her legs felt as if they would fail.

"At least he went peacefully, didn't he?" she said to Marlowe as they looked at the coffin, far below. "He was smiling. I'm glad for that."

That was because he thought I was on his side, thought Marlowe. *But many wagers are placed in the Otherworld, and Edward's luck was better in death than in life. An Intermediary can be bought by a rich soul, just like anyone else. Can't they, Mr Dobbs Senior?*

She resisted the temptation, the wicked urge, to tell Rachel what awaited her husband, instead saying, "The last thing he saw was you, my dear. Why wouldn't he smile?"

And inside the coffin lay Eddy in his good suit. Around his neck—above the well starched collar of his best shirt, was the iron band with the spikes pointing outwards. For now. His left hand was contained in an iron-banded cage, his father's sovereign ring on the third finger so it could be returned to its owner. And on his testicles was clamped the iron box; the small hole in the top designed to pour water in before the box, and its contents, were heated to boiling point.

All the instruments were ready for use. And would be used. For aeons.

Scar Tissue

One on the palm of her hand, an inch long, from a deep cut. Accidental; made by falling onto a sharp stone. Three on her shoulder blade, longer, but superficial. Deliberate; scarification. One on her knee, rounded, from the removal of skin. Accidental; from a school hockey match. One on her neck, a straight line from head to shoulders. Accidental; a cat scratch. One on her upper arm, jagged and wide, still delicate looking despite its age, the skin stretched and bumpy. Misadventure; falling from a tree onto barbed wire.

The chaffinch's song stopped the conversation then helped to restart it. They could hear the bird as soon as Case opened the window. She spotted it in the tree outside, and its song began before she'd sat back down with the others, Bella, her long-time flatmate and Marie, the new woman, just moved in.

They listened to the bird for a while, its chirping song on endless repeat. For a moment Hackney Downs could have been in the middle of the countryside.

"I think it's amazing," said Case. "That tiny bird! Its song sounds complicated but it never seems to get it wrong."

"I've meditated to birdsong before," said Bella. The others laughed. "I'm serious. The repeating patterns are brilliant to focus on."

Marie slowly shook her head. "Sorry, not

impressed. Yes, it must be very strong to sing at that volume, but it keeps doing the same thing. If it changed its song it would have an advantage on the other chaffinches. Wouldn't it?"

They talked for a while longer then Marie suddenly said, "Case, where did you get that scar on the back of your neck?"

It was a bold question. Most people politely ignored such things but Marie was already proving to be not like most people.

"There's no dramatic story behind it," Case replied. "My aunt's cat did it. It was having a mad half hour and jumped on me. I like that scar! It's nearly thirty years old now."

Bella began to laugh. "Do you remember when the landlord saw it? He was really suspicious."

"He assumed I'd got it in a knife fight," said Case. "Like some hoodlum from the 1950s. Thought I might be too dodgy to rent to."

"So stupid," said Bella. "We all have scars, don't we?"

Marie stared at her. Eventually she asked what the landlord, Griffin, was like, having only met him once.

"Old fashioned. Conservative. A prat," said Case. "Just don't give him a reason to be pissed off. Luckily we don't see him very often."

And all the while, the chaffinch sang.

The weeks passed. The three women barely saw each other for days at a time. Case, especially, was busy studying, which she was grateful for, as it gave her less time to mope over her recent breakup. But there were times at home when she was able to talk to Marie and try to get to know her, although it seemed to Case that the more she discovered about the woman, the more confused she became. Every answer Marie gave raised more questions.

When Bella had said that everyone had scars, Case had agreed; after all, on a physical, emotional and philosophical level, everyone's lives left marks on them. Some covered the visible ones with clothing, others more permanently, with tattoos, too far removed from their experiences to want to be reminded of them. But some were as honest as Case, happy to reveal life's misadventures.

Marie was different. She had no scars.

A conversation with her would begin ordinarily enough, but then it would be revealed that she had done a little more than everyone else. As a child she had climbed bigger trees but had never fallen from one, she'd ridden her bike faster and further than anyone else, but had never crashed it. Whenever she'd slipped in life, she'd landed on her feet, unhurt. She'd survived her childhood unscathed.

She told amazing tales of her adult life, too. Case heard excerpts, either from Marie herself or from an awe-struck Bella. Marie had moved to London from Manchester, a city that Marie dismissed in a sentence (*"Done the clubs, slept with the women, got fed up with the rain,"*), presumably because she had lived in so many other, more exotic places: on a kibbutz in Israel, as a fire eater in Greece, as a photographer's assistant in San Francisco. The woman's life was a tapestry of adventure. Case was at first amazed by her stories but as time went on they became confusing. Apart from a timeline that twisted and turned, to have had so many daring exploits but no memento of any of them seemed impossible. It wouldn't be the first time; Case had met liars and showoffs before, but they had been easily found out. Such people were transparent, desperate to create their own mythology, whereas Marie was so strong, so plausible. And she made no effort to cover her body. Her vest tops and short skirts revealed no scars, no tattoos, not even a vaccination mark. Case felt flawed in comparison. For a moment she even wondered if her own scars were symbols of weakness and felt angry for doubting herself. Did Marie look down on the rest of the world, so full of what she considered as imperfection? Case got the feeling that she did. Did men find her as threatening as women found her attractive, more dangerous for a lifetime of perfection? But it was strength that made a person get back on a bike after they'd fallen off, strength that made them learn from their mistakes. How could someone who had never failed be trusted? Bella clearly adored Marie and refused to find fault with her. In a strange way, Case understood, it felt wrong to question anything Marie said, so she kept her disquiet to herself. How could someone who had never failed be trusted? And the woman had only just moved to London. Perhaps Marie was simply on her guard, cautious about what she gave away.

There were noises coming from the next room, the sound of Marie dressing filtering through the thin wall. Case suddenly thought of Marie's unmarked body, perhaps naked as she rummaged through her wardrobe just a few inches away. She extinguished the vision; it made her feel equally predatory and ridiculous. If Marie was perfect then she was also unattainable and should, according to Case's own philosophy, be uninteresting.

But she was making friends; all of Bella and Case's circle thought she was remarkable, and she inspired people to take her into their confidence.

Marie's opinion, her approval, was vital. Even Case had done it. Still grieving over her failed relationship, she had come home one night and told Marie all about it, something she was beginning to regret. It was a sad tale. Katie's parents had been drinkers. Her father would get violent, her mother emotional and clingy. Katie called them Nice Cop and Nasty Cop; both had different methods of making her confess to any crime they dreamt up. Katie had a scar over one eye, another behind her ear and several on the backs of her thighs, all inflicted by her father. She had several others, the results of normal childhood scrapes. Case had liked those ones, cherishing how they felt, what they stood for. The others just made her angry and upset. She'd tried kissing them better, loving Katie fiercely, imagining it could be enough to make them heal. But they didn't disappear and they never would; they were, after all, like details of a map, the cartography of Katie's life. But Katie was too damaged to be in a relationship, and Case had often wondered how she felt when heat made the bad scars itch or the sun made them stand out, like a diary that constantly falls open on the wrong page.

Another month passed. Marie was faultless and fun. Case warmed to her, dismissing her suspicions about the woman as pure envy. One rainy afternoon, Case was in the lounge, reading, when she heard Marie coming up the stairs, talking excitedly and then a second female voice, laughing in response. They went into Marie's room, the murmur of voices continuing. There was less and less talk and then the sounds became unclear. Case unconsciously listened harder, trying to make out what was going on. Then came the unmistakable sound of the pair heading for bed. And

Case recognised the second voice. It was Bella. Case silently cursed the pair of them. Flatmates sleeping together never ended well. She put the television on, slightly too loud for comfort. Eventually she went for a walk. It was best just to be out of the way.

The week was busy. Case was at the University all day and spent her evenings away from the house. She had no time to dwell on Marie and saw no sign of her until the next weekend.

It was to be two days that turned the world upside down.

On that Saturday morning. Case was up early. She was expecting a letter from a friend overseas. She showered and dressed and made her way downstairs just as the post was pushed through the letterbox. She sorted the letters, took her own and was on her way back to her room when there was a crash from the kitchen. The door was open a crack and she looked through, stopping short without entering. Marie was in there, and Case was reluctant to join her unless she really needed help. Marie was bending over, picking something up from the floor. She'd evidently dropped a vase. Chunks of glass were scattered around. and as Marie went to pick them up she slipped. She held up her hand; a jagged, cruel looking shard stuck out.

My God! A mistake! thought Case.

Marie regarded it for a moment and then slowly pulled the razor sharp piece out, leaving a deep gash in her hand. Blood poured down her arm and splattered onto the floor. Case watched, the sight turning her stomach. Marie's hand was a mess. She needed to go to hospital. Case was about to walk in and offer to call for an ambulance, but something about the way Marie was reacting made her hang back.

She did not seem to be at all disturbed, or in pain, just captivated with what was happening. As Case looked, the wound stopped bleeding. The torn, bloody skin stretched. One side of the wound reached out to the other. When the sides touched they grasped each other, knitted themselves together and in the space of a few minutes Marie's hand was healed. When the process was finished she washed the blood off her arm and the floor. There was nothing to show what had happened, and there would certainly be no scar. She continued clearing up the broken glass, wrapped it in newspaper and put it in the bin. Case crept off.

How had Marie managed such a feat? Case had heard of wise women and healers doing things that were rubbished by modern medicine, mocked as fraud or wishful thinking, but although she believed that some things were possible with faith and ancient knowledge, she had never seen a healer in action or heard of anything as dramatic as what had just happened. Things were now even more bewildering than before. After a few hours, though, the incident seemed unreal. She tried to make some notes about it, but when she read them back they sounded ridiculous. She wished she had gone straight into the kitchen, She would have been more sure about what had occurred. She could talk to Marie about it but she wanted to find out more before questioning her.

That evening there was a knock on her door. It was Marie, holding a bottle of wine and two glasses.

"Want to share this? Or have you got something better to do?"

There was the slightest hint of mockery in Marie's voice. Case stared at her, looking for a sign that what she had seen that morning had really happened. But nothing was out of the ordinary. At a loss for anything to say, she let Marie in.

They talked. At first it was just gossip, who was going out with who. After a few drinks Marie suddenly began talking about the woman she had slept with the week before. "The woman" was just a friend, she said. It had been nothing serious, just some fun. Case shrugged and said it was none of her business. Deep down, she felt relieved. But she wondered why Marie had told her; was she trying to find out whether if Bella had talked? Or was she boasting?

While she frowned and tried to work things out, Marie leant forward and kissed her. Case, fairly drunk by this time, was caught completely off guard. But she was in no state to question Marie's actions and was certainly not going to resist her. Besides, this was her chance to find out more. She put down her glass.

Marie's body was astonishing. Case kissed every inch of it, ran her fingers along every contour, searching. She needed to find something, anything, but there was not as much as a stretch mark on her body. The woman was unmapped. She had no record of her own history. It was too weird. Case stopped.

She apologised, blaming the wine. Marie stroked Case's face with the hand that she'd injured so badly that morning. She didn't flinch or move it awkwardly. It was as if nothing had happened.

"Doesn't it hurt? Your hand, I mean. I saw you cut it on some glass this morning," Case blurted out. She didn't want to wonder about it any more.

"I knew someone was spying on me." Marie said coldly as she got dressed. "You've seen my hands. There's not a mark on them. Maybe you were imagining things this morning. Or maybe I just wasn't hurt enough for it to show."

And that was all she would say. Case felt she was being taunted, retaliation for her apparent disinterest, something Marie clearly wasn't used to. Was she playing a game of some kind, an attempt to pit her flatmates against one another? Or was it really just fun, with no hidden agenda? Case could not believe she had come to her because of a serious attraction; quite frankly, she was too safe for Marie. Made cautious by life, she had once been described as a bird with one wing clipped, an analogy Case had reluctantly agreed with. But once Case was alone again, more pressing questions came to mind. After the conversation they'd had about that morning, she was now certain of what she'd seen. What remained was how it could have happened.

Could someone simply *refuse* to be scarred? Could they deny injury to such an extent that it could be reversed? Was it possible to have such strength of will, for the mind to have such control over matter? Whatever the answer, Marie possessed phenomenal powers. How had she learnt them? What was the truth of her past? And why would someone so astonishing be living with her and Bella? The flat was big but had never been well maintained by the landlord, and on winter days like these was cold and damp. It was too *ordinary* for Marie. Case had lived there for nearly three years; her lowly income from working in the student shop and bar kept her on the poverty line, but she liked the familiarity of the place. It was home. On the days that she saw neither of the others the space yawned luxuriously around her.

Case tried to put Marie out of her mind, but was finding it impossible. Over the last few days she had rearranged her room, moving her bed to the connecting wall and putting her desk closer to the door so she would see Marie as she entered or left. She began to watch her closely and spent long hours listening to her in her room. She knew what music she liked, which television shows she watched, who she phoned. Ashamed and quite disturbed by her increasing obsession, she kept promising herself that tomorrow it would stop and everything would go back to normal. But stopping was so difficult. She had seen Marie once or twice at home but they had spoken no more than a few words. Case dared do no more than exchange small talk, but at the same time having no proper contact with her, to not even discuss what had happened between them, was unbearable and one night a few days later she found herself following Marie when she went out. Marie walked through Mare Street and towards London Fields, confident in what was an unsafe neighbourhood at that time of day. Finally, she stopped at a door next to a rundown clothing factory, pressed a bell and went inside. The house and the street were unfamiliar. Case went home. The temptation to enter Marie's room, to search for a clue as to her past, was almost overwhelming but she resisted it.

When Marie left the house again the next afternoon, Case followed but lost her down the twisting passageways that cut from the Downs to the churchyard in the centre of Hackney. When she caught up with Marie again, she was not alone. She was standing in the late afternoon gloom, face to face with a hooded figure. Case could not hear the conversation but it was obvious what it was about; a man was demanding money. Marie laughed defiantly and went to walk on, but the man grabbed her and punched her in the stomach, knocking her to the ground. He bent down and began rifling through her coat pockets. Case ran from her hiding place, shouting as loudly as she could and the man ran off, whether empty-handed or not, Case couldn't tell. She was more concerned for Marie, who was still lying on the ground. The flagstones glistened around her and to Case's horror she realised Marie had been stabbed. Judging by the amount of blood, it was serious. She carefully raised Marie's shirt, meaning to cover the wound but as she gazed at the terrible injury the impossible happened again.

The flow of blood began to reverse.

Case watched in astonishment as Marie's body struggled against the injury. The blood that covered the pavement worked its way back into her stomach, cleaning itself of mud, grit and other impurities as it went. The wound opened up to let the blood back in, enough for Case to witness the miracle of Marie's body repairing itself. When all the blood was gone and the internal injuries healed, the flaps of the cut in her stomach rippled and grew. New skin made its way across the wound and the deep cut disappeared. When it was over Marie began to stir, and Case ran away.

Case went to the pub, smoked a rare cigarette and had a drink but no answers came to her. She was leaving when she heard Mancunian accents behind her and turned back. There was a couple at the bar who she didn't recognise. They were fairly drunk but seemed good-natured with it. The gay scene being what it was—like a small village even in most cities—it was worth talking to them. Case walked over and asked if either of them had known Marie.

Both were bemused until Case showed them the photo of Marie she had on her phone.

"That's Zoe! There was a rumour she'd changed her name. How do you know her?"

"She's my new flatmate," said Case. "Are you friends of hers?"

The women laughed and crossed themselves theatrically.

"You poor bitch! Zoe's fucked up. She ran away from Manchester when things stopped going her way. So this is where she ended up."

"If she's here we might get the next train back home."

Case wished they were sober. She wanted reliable information. "So you're not friends? It's just that her stories don't really add up."

"Oh, they do," said the older of the women. "If she's lived about two hundred years, that is. Done a lot, hasn't she?" She grabbed Case's arm. "Be careful. Just don't get too involved with her. She doesn't know the difference between fantasy and reality and I don't think it's the first time she's changed her name. There's something wrong about that, isn't there?"

Case left the pub and went home to find Bella, about to leave for her night shift, in tears.

"Griffin turned up out of the blue! And Marie was in her room, smoking a joint. She didn't even try to disguise the smell. He went mad. He's evicting her."

Bella hadn't spoken to Marie, who had stayed in her room, or Griffin, who had stamped out, but was desperate at the prospect of Marie having to leave. Case calmed her down and shooed her out, then went to her room to think. Despite the warnings from the women in the pub—who could easily have their own agenda—Case was panic stricken. There had to be a way to stop this; she had to talk Griffin round. Case had discovered something miraculous about Marie, far beyond Bella's romantic yearnings. She needed to be part of Marie's life.

She took some deep breaths and listened; Marie would surely call a friend to find somewhere to stay, at least temporarily. Something like this, she thought, would never faze her. But as she sat there she heard Marie muttering a desperate mantra: *"It was supposed to be safe here."* It went on for several minutes before stopping. There was silence for a while, then....what? A sound. Soft; a sigh? Another, a low moan, the sound of someone in pain, suffering quietly.

The sounds were frightening. Had she done something terrible to herself? Case hesitated, still not wanting to intrude but knowing she had to do something. Finally she went to Marie's room and knocked gently on the door.

"Marie? It's Case. Are you alright?"

There was no answer. She knocked again and then went in.

Marie was standing by her bed, motionless, in a trance. She was naked. Her head was thrown back to face the ceiling but her eyes were glazed over and she saw nothing. Her arms were stretched out in front of her, the muscles taut and raised. Her mouth opened and a low monotone began that sounded as if it would never end. It was distorted, so unlike Marie's voice that an insane thought, that the woman was possessed by something supernatural, crossed Case's mind.

To her relief, the sound became muffled. Case moved closer. There was something moving inside her, in her oesophagus. Her neck bulged as the obstruction made its way up her throat, and then it appeared at the back of her mouth. Her vocal chords now unobstructed, the horrible monotone began again. Case tried to ignore the sound and looked closely at what was inside her mouth. It was a ball of white matter. As she watched, thin pieces pulled away from the mass. They crept slowly to her lips, hesitated, then continued, out into the room. Blind, wormlike, they tentatively felt their way, hanging in the air as more of the stuff left Marie's nostrils, twisting languidly into strange shapes.

It looked like ectoplasm, the scene like a gothic Victorian séance. *Was* Marie possessed? The thought was no longer mad. Case wanted to help her, but didn't want to hurt her. And she realised, to her shame, that she was afraid, not just of what was happening, but also of *her*, of Marie. Case watched Marie's chest rise and fall as she breathed. She was alive, although how aware she was of what was happening Case could not guess. Her gaze returned to the white matter. She carefully reached out to touch the lengths that hung before her. She ran a finger along the twists and turns. To her surprise, it was a familiar feeling. The matter was made of stretched skin, bumpy and uneven with a few light hairs growing at awkward angles from the edges. Case recognised it. No ectoplasm, this.

They were scars.

Where had the stuff come from? Had it entered her from the attack a few hours before, or had Marie always kept it inside her, like a ball of wool that was now becoming unravelled? With no scars of her own, did she have a way of gathering them from other people?

Case stood there, transfixed by the scene. For a while she was as motionless as Marie. For all her fear, the room was calm and still and she didn't want to disturb it. A sudden sound, of something tearing, snapped Case out of her trance. She looked frantically around, trying to locate its source, before her eyes settled on Marie's inner thigh. The skin had split; there was a line from her groin to her ankle. The sound began again, like the ripping of heavy material. There was no blood, just a neat, straight line that passed under her foot and up the other side of her leg to her hip. When it was done, the other thigh tore in the same way.

Marie was oblivious. She remained staring upwards, the scarred skin still hanging in the air. The tearing stopped. The flesh around her legs fell away and flopped to the floor. Case gagged, expecting to see all kinds of gore, but what was there was worse.

Underneath the skin was another pair of legs.

They were long and slender, the skin ebony black and unblemished. Marie's head straightened. Soon she was facing forward again. The scars slowly found their way back into her nose and mouth. When it was gone she fell to her knees and then forward, onto her face. The skin on the rest of her body began to ripple, each wave moving it slowly along, away from the new body lying underneath. It was as intense as a birth. It made Case think of an insect leaving a cocoon.

She covered her mouth to stop herself from screaming and stepped back into the shadowed corner of the room. Marie appeared incapable of seeing or hearing, but Case was not going to take chances. She had been right to be afraid after all.

Finally the flesh that Case had known as Marie dropped away to the floor. A tall, African woman stood up in her place. She was pierced at the eyebrow, the nose, the lip, the nipples and navel, her head shaved to near baldness. Her body glistened, wet as a newborn. She breathed in deeply, took Marie's towel and wiped herself dry. Then she quickly dressed. Marie's clothes were ill-fitting on her new, taller, body, but they were enough to cover her. She walked past Case and out of the room.

Case waited, terrified, listening to the footsteps walking down the stairs and out of the flat. She was alone again. She waited a little longer and then cautiously approached Marie's body which lay, discarded, on the floor. The skin, so warm and smooth when she'd caressed it a few days before, held all the sensation of plastic, a dead thing. But it was not a corpse she was touching; this was so much less than that. It was just a shell. Case turned it over, unable to ignore Marie's flattened and expressionless face, and looked inside. It was not a gruesome sight; it was too pristine. There were no blood, or bones, or guts to contend with. It was clean and dry and utterly grotesque.

The shell was not entirely empty. Scores of white lines ran around the inside of Marie's body. They were chaotic, criss-crossing one another over and over again, fighting for space. In some places there was so much of the stuff that it hung down like empty washing lines. Case reached in and felt them. She began counting the layers but there were so many she gave up. At last, she had the beginnings of an answer.

All the stories Marie had told, all the places she'd claimed to have been and the things she said she'd done, all were likely to be true. But her claim to never have been hurt enough for it to show was a lie. Marie had been made of scar tissue. Scars upon scars upon scars; the memories of a million wounds. She must have experienced more pain than Case could possibly imagine. She had hidden them, tucked them away, in a place so deep inside that no one would ever see them, to be discarded with her old skin when the wounds overwhelmed her and she had needed to begin again. Case had no doubt now that they were her own, that the pain that had created them was hers alone. Marie's body had not been able to bear any more pain and so she had become someone else.

So what was she? A natural aberration, a scientific experiment? Or something simpler, more tragic, a normal human being who had evolved into something else out of necessity? Had her life been so dreadful, so cruel, that to be herself was just too painful? Either way, Case supposed, it amounted to the same thing. She was a monster.

Case sank to the floor and cried for her.

The front gate clanged shut. Whoever, whatever, Marie had become was out in an unsuspecting world.

Theophany

He had wanted to enter at Traitors' Gate.

It would have been more appropriate, but it was impractical, and so Christopher Sun reluctantly opted for the main entrance. He paid his admission fee and walked through. The Tower of London, always one of his favourite places, was comparatively quiet although he guessed there were still a couple of hundred people milling around. A woman with two children stood nearby. She was reading from the guide book.

"You see that raven? There are seven of them living here now and they protect the Tower. Legend says the Tower will fall if the ravens leave."

Oh yes, thought Sun. *The Tower and the Kingdom both.*

He followed the little family as they wandered the grounds. It was nearly midday; time, then. A sudden commotion, the flapping of a dozen wings, made the family look up.

"The ravens!" said the boy. "They're flying away."

His mother laughed and counted the birds. "It's alright. It's only six of them. There's still another one here somewhere."

The six birds flew away, over the wall and towards the Thames. Sun began to walk, covering the open ground quickly and reached the White Tower, standing as close to it as he could. The seventh raven hopped along the ground. Sun held out an arm and the raven flew up to sit on it.

The family turned and watched, the children squealing at the sight of the raven perched on Sun's arm. He smiled at them and threw the bird towards the sky. It opened its wings and flew, circled for a while, then was over the wall and away.

"Who'll fall?" he called. *"Who'll fall?"*

The earth split in front of him. The fault line ran out towards the family. The woman grabbed her children, dragged them across the widening gap and clutched them to her side. Then the ground beneath them dropped away and they disappeared without as much as a scream between them.

Sun took a quick glance around. All the buildings inside the Tower walls were crumbling, the ground around them opening up and swallowing rubble and groups of tourists. Police and Beefeaters ran through the gates and straight into the chasm. One Beefeater, looking frankly ridiculous in traditional costume and designer spectacles, caught Sun's eye for a second before he disappeared.

He leant back, pushing firmly against the reassuring strength of the White Tower. As promised, it was the only safe place within the Tower's walls. It was like standing on a cliff edge. Only inches in front of him was nothingness.

One step forward and he would drop all the way to the darkworlds.

On the other side of the Tower's walls, he knew that life would be continuing as normal. Perhaps someone had heard screaming, the rumble of collapsing stone and earth, and had called the emergency services. But there was no wail of sirens, not yet.

He sidestepped around the Tower, turned a corner with difficulty and found, to his relief, that the timber steps leading to the entrance were still intact. He scrambled gratefully onto them and went through the door.

The inside of the White Tower no longer existed. In the space of a few minutes the Keep had gone, leaving only the walls with their austere turrets and the roof. The building's new dimensions brought with it new acoustics; every breath that Sun took seemed to bounce off the walls and down into the chasm. A thin curtain of dust filled the building, catching the sunlight that made its way through the windows. And that was not all. Sun leant forward and looked down. At the centre of the chasm was blackness and slowly rising dust but despite the chaos someone had been busy.

There were ladders propped around the sides of the opening. Sun crept forward, testing the ground with each step before putting his full weight down. He counted a dozen ladders of varying length; some reached halfway up the empty building, others barely made it to ground level. The ladders were products of the darkworlds, of that Sun had no doubt; who from up here would want to climb down *there?* Even Sun had no intention of doing that. Most were clearly made from bones lashed together with skin and sinew. Another was of a material Sun didn't recognise. When he reached out and touched it, it shifted under his hand. Whatever it was, it was still alive. In the furthest corner of the void, he noticed something else; narrow stone steps leading down. They looked crudely made, or perhaps were so old and well used that they'd worn away. Sun was on his way over to investigate further when a sound, just the hint of a sound, really, stopped him. He could hear footsteps. They were way, way off in the distance, but it was unmistakeably the sound of shoe upon stone.

Someone was walking up the steps. Christopher Sun retreated to the darkest of the shadows and waited.

Up and up. It seemed he had been walking *up* forever. The steps hugged the walls of the abyss and appeared, in the gloom, to run back into themselves. It was like being on Escher's *Endless Staircase*, forever climbing but going nowhere.

Was that a metaphor for his life? Martin Witter wasn't sure and it was academic anyway; it had been a long time since he'd been alive. All there was was the staircase and the need to get to the top, if such a place existed. Witter was a broken man in every way. Ten years ago he'd had everything and was about to accumulate even more, but then he had been hurled into the darkworlds and the hands of the masters. They had taken him apart. Not in the furious, bloodthirsty way he had expected of those he had tried to double-cross, but calmly, deliberately. He had been completely shattered, reassembled in a way that had pleased the masters, and then sent back up to a world he barely believed had ever really existed, to do the masters' bidding.

From the outside, Witter looked much the same as he ever had, although on closer inspection tiny lines could be seen all over his skin, like cracks on ancient ceramics. It was on the inside where everything was different. Organs, bones and veins had been rearranged. His heart sat in his bowels, his lungs nearly choked him as they fought for space in his oesophagus. His physical rewiring made functioning almost impossible, but it was his mind that was most damaged. It had been pulverised, not only by the masters, but by what he had seen in the darkworlds. The knowledge that his son, Boyd, had actively sought the place out, had spend years trying to find it, and then had romped through it, revelling in its disgusting, terrifying extremes, was the worst thing of all. He had loved and hated Boyd equally, a constant tug-of-war of emotion. Having to dump Boyd's broken body into the mighty, stinking River Thames was the final, heartbreaking straw at the time but now, seeing that he had escaped the mighty, stinking darkworlds, Witter blessed the act.

And still he climbed the steps. His legs, broken in a hundred places, the bones jumbled up and put back together, felt as if they would collapse at any moment, but they held him upright as he finally made his way into sunlight and fresh air.

He stepped onto ground level and stopped to rest, taking in small gulps of air. He did not recognise where he was, although he knew he must be in central London, for that was where his mission lay. The building he had entered was a shell, old stone walls grandly protecting nothing less than the arsehole of Hell. Although the place proclaimed itself empty, Witter sensed a presence. Which was as it should be; he was supposed to be met. When he'd finally got his breath back he whispered into the dusty air.

"Christopher Sun! Show yourself. I'm not to be kept waiting."

His worlds bounced across the expanse of stone, gaining momentum as they went. After a moment, Christopher Sun stepped out from the shadows. Sun held his smile as he approached Martin Witter, a man who had once been so powerful, so privileged. Now he was a shambles. Thus was the result of trying to outwit the masters. Witter stared blankly at Sun's outstretched hand, as if he'd never seen such a gesture before. Sun put his hand down.

"It's good to see you, Mr Witter," he said. "So much has happened since you went away. Perhaps you've heard of The Association?"

Sun paused, long enough to enjoy the glazed expression on Witter's face, then continued. "Of course you have. That's why the masters sent you back up here. We're to meet with them."

Witter took a step towards the open door. Sun grasped the place where his shoulder should have been; there was bone and flesh there but *that* was no shoulder blade.

"Not yet," said Sun. "It's busy out there. We must bide our time. We wait until nightfall."

The latest news, even on the Internet, was that there was no latest news. Disaster on a huge scale had befallen the Tower of London; the land inside the Tower's walls had collapsed, taking the buildings, most of the staff and all of the two hundred and twenty three visitors who had been inside, with it. No rescue attempt had yet been made; the area was now a huge chasm, so deep it was not possible to see the bottom, and until the ground around the Tower was deemed to be safe, no one could go near it. A police helicopter had made numerous passes overhead, and although it appeared that the distinctive walls and turrets of the Keep had miraculously remained intact, there was no sign of life, The chasm would be investigated once it had been decided how to do so.

Early speculation was that an earthquake or natural fault in the ground below the Tower was to blame, or possibly even a meteor falling to Earth. Reports that the famous ravens had flown away shortly before the tragedy were being dismissed as hysteria. The Prime Minister would be making a statement later.

"Just as soon as you've got any idea of what to say," murmured Cara Limehouse. "If only you could blame it on terrorists."

The event had been shocking but it was the reference to the legend of the ravens' departure from the Tower that had caught Cara's attention. She signed in to one of the forums she frequented. As she suspected, a discussion regarding the ravens was taking place.

"Ravens were seen flying away from the Tower about five minutes before the disaster," 'Roger's Folly' had posted. "There is some dispute over how many. Most witnesses think there were six."

"If that was the case," she contributed under her username 'Spyglass', "then the legend wasn't the cause. There have been seven resident ravens for some time. Saying that, a single raven flying wouldn't have been noticed. It could have happened."

A private message appeared almost immediately: *Hello, Spyglass! Do you believe any of this stuff?* It was signed 'Sasquatch'. Cara had never met anyone on the forum, but was inclined to trust a few of them. Sasquatch, as far as Cara had worked out, was a woman from Canada who was equally open-minded and sceptical about everything. Cara replied to the message: *Why not? It makes as much sense as any other explanation. It certainly wasn't an earthquake.*

Their conversation was suddenly interrupted when a new private message appeared in the corner of Cara's screen.

All of the ravens left the Tower one minute before its collapse. This was to create a route out of the darkworlds. The Association is to blame. Martin Witter has been returned. Disorder will follow and the whole world shall fall if the chasm remains. The ravens must be brought back to the Tower.

It was signed 'Eternal Traveller', a name Cara was not familiar with from the forum. Intrigued, she asked the newcomer who they were.

All in good time, came the reply. *If you want confirmation of what I've told you, be at Traitors' Gate at 2 a.m. and remain well hidden. Everything you dream is real.*

With that, the Eternal Traveller went offline, but a file had been attached to the message. Cara scanned it for viruses but it was clean, so she opened it up. It contained a collection of newspaper articles. Several were reports of brutal murders and two reported the disappearance of a wealthy businessman called Martin Witter shortly after the disappearance of his rather wayward son, Boyd. Cara could find no link between any of the stories other than that they dated from late in 2002 and all related to events in London. She saved the file and went back to her conversation with Sasquatch.

Just had the strangest chat, with 'Eternal Traveller'. Do you know him/her? They want me to go to the Tower in the early hours. Apparently I'll see what caused the disaster.

Sasquatch was as sceptical as Cara guessed she'd be: *This sounds like a terrible experience waiting to happen,* she wrote. *Don't go!*

Hmm. But what if it's not? Cara replied. *I'll think about it. And I won't approach anyone who I couldn't beat in a fight.*

Sasquatch urged Cara to change her mind, but something the Eternal Traveller had said had taken root.

Everything you dream is real.

This was the thing she'd always hoped for, and the thing she most dreaded.

She slept through the first part of the night but woke before the alarm and splashed water over her greying, cropped hair to wake herself fully. Then she dressed and cycled to what was left of the Tower of London, stopping a discreet distance away in order to approach the ruin quietly.

Barriers had been erected around the perimeter. A sleepy looking security guard made his way around but the area was desolate and he disappeared, stifling a yawn as he went. Cara made her way towards Traitors' Gate and hid behind a large plane tree. No one was around, of that she was sure.

Not on land, anyway. The nearby Thames suddenly splashed against the bank, as if a boat was passing by, although the rest of the river was silent. Not wanting to miss whatever might happen at the Tower, Cara risked a glance behind her.

A figure was climbing up from the water. Cara couldn't tell if it was male or female. As it strode towards her she could see water falling from it, not dripping as it would from soaked clothing or skin, but in blobs, repelled, as it would be from a duck's feathers.

"Spyglass!" it whispered cheerily, as if they were old friends.

Cara stood her ground, noting which was the best direction for escape should it be needed. The figure smiled as it reached her, and Cara almost relaxed. It was female. Probably.

"Eternal Traveller? I'm Cara. What's your real-life name?"

The figure raised its eyebrows. "I don't have a real-life name, basically because I'm neither real nor alive. Not in any way you'd recognise. But when I *was* alive I was a woman who contracted smallpox. In London, in this century. Now I travel; endlessly."

Cara opened her mouth to pour scorn on the claim but looked again at the woman's strange features and completely dry hair and clothes. She couldn't think of anything to say, so said nothing.

The woman looked up at the stars. "It must be close to two o'clock. We need to get closer to the Gate. You *must* see what's about to happen."

They hurried across the open space to the barrier and looked through the remains of the Gate to the yawning chasm and the bizarre sight of the White Tower, seemingly complete, standing alone.

"What about the security guard? He'll be back here any time," said Cara.

"Oh, you won't see him again. He'll be dead by now," said the Eternal Traveller.

Cara waited for an explanation but none was forthcoming. She stared across at the White Tower and willed nothing to happen.

"Death is pain!" spat Martin Witter.

Christopher Sun shook his head. "Death is peace," he said. "Moving on, perhaps, but with all our shackles removed. Such luxury! You are in pain because you're *not* dead."

"I'm not alive, you fool," hissed Witter through his tombstone teeth. "How could I be after what *they* put me through?"

"They put you through what you deserved to be put through," said Sun, nervous at any mention of the masters. "And you're not dead but you're certainly not alive. You're neither here nor there."

Witter turned to him. "And who are you, anyway? Are you one of them? One of those freaks?"

"No, I'm not one of them. Perhaps one day I will be," said Sun. "But they trust me. That's why I'm here."

Witter sneered. "You're a wannabe. My son was one of those. He *liked* it down there." He coughed, then gave a sob of pain as his lungs tried to force themselves further up his throat.

Sun felt a passing moment of pity for the wreckage of a man, but motioned for him to be silent. They needed to cross the outer chasm and meet with The Association. Sun could hear movement but was unsure where it was coming from; outside the White Tower or from below. He listened intently.

Movement was coming from both places.

The sound of large wings beating came from outside the door. Then the creaking of weight on the wooden steps. Something bent low to get through the door. At the same time a figure came rushing up the bone ladder.

While Witter looked on without emotion, Sun tried desperately to hide his.

Two creatures from the darkworlds were in the building with them.

Both, admittedly, were hideous; part animal, part devil, one stinking and shitting itself, the other—the one that had flown down from doing God knew what outside—bathed in fresh blood. They were creatures that had seen and done unimaginable things. And now, Sun assumed, they were here as transport across the outer chasm. He pointed at the shitting creature.

"You take Witter," he said and turned away.

Martin Witter's further humiliation was not necessary to see. The other creature shook some of the blood off its face and grasped Sun tightly with claws that felt like nails. It opened its wings and flew clumsily through the door, catching Sun on the solid stonework before heading outside and over the outer wall. Sun, barely conscious, collapsed where he was dropped. The smell of shit woke him up. Witter had been placed next to him and the two creatures were already heading towards the White Tower and presumably back to the darkworlds.

While Cara Limehouse, jaw sagging, watched the two men being deposited rudely on the ground, the Eternal Traveller merely sighed in resignation. Cara turned to her, her face full of questions. She had seen the men get up and walk away; one, in obvious pain, had been easily recognisable as Martin Witter.

"He was in the file you sent," she whispered. "I'd assumed he was dead. Where's he been all this time? He looks terrible."

"I expect he wishes he was dead," said the Eternal Traveller. "Cara, you're going to have to accept what you see. There's not enough time in the world to explain everything. This is what you need to know…"

The Eternal Traveller told Cara of the darkworlds, the bartering Witter had been doing with the masters, his underestimation of them and his plan to wipe them out and sell the darkworlds. She spoke of its horrifying inhabitants that had roamed on Earth, in London, at the time; the Torquis, Roi O'Hanlon, and Yellow Jack, the creature that had brushed his hand against her own one terrible day ten years ago on Tower Bridge and gave her the disease that killed her.

"What you won't find in the file," she said, "are

the cases, the cluster of the worst diseases known to humankind that suddenly afflicted hundreds of Londoners a decade ago. What the authorities never found was the link, that all of those people had been walking across Tower Bridge late in the afternoon of the 23rd of September 2002. Yellow Jack infected them all, purely for his own amusement."

"So what's happening now?" asked Cara. Who or what had transported the two men from the remains of the Tower of London would have to wait for as long as she could bear.

"Martin Witter and the other man, Christopher Sun, are going to a meeting. Believe me, it's not as banal as it sounds. We won't be following; we have a more important task. The inner chasm, the one inside the White Tower, cannot be allowed to remain, the Tower of London must be restored. And there's only one way to do that."

The Eternal Traveller looked up into the trees that lined the riverbank.

"The ravens must be returned to the Tower."

Cara laughed, not caring who heard. Track down seven wild birds in a population of who knew how many? The enormity of the task was hilarious.

"We'll go out at dawn and call them by name, shall we? Oh, and while we're at it, you can tell me why you've chosen me to do the impossible."

In response, the Eternal Traveller opened her mouth. A flicker of light like a flaming tongue poked out. The light fanned and enveloped first her head, then her whole body.

It was not only light, but energy. It consumed Cara for no more than a moment, but it was enough to leave her reeling and emotional, enough to send tears streaming down her cheeks. The light was

Life, the energy was the spirit of Everything. Every animal, every blade of grass, the sea, the stars, the air she breathed. Dizzy, she staggered and fell in an undignified heap to the ground. When she'd recovered enough to get up, the Eternal Traveller was back to her normal self.

"Wonderful, isn't it?" she said. "The places we go to when we die! But there's only so much I'm capable of like this. I need some help. You've experienced many things in your lifetime. You're far more powerful than you know; you can't expect to go through life without picking up an enchantment or two."

In which case, one enchantment was surely what she'd just experienced; the knowledge of what she would become when her life ended.

The meeting with The Association was set for ten o'clock. There was plenty of time to get them both rested and cleaned up, but Christopher Sun kept Witter moving, or more accurately, shambling through the City streets for several hours, only relenting to stop and buy them both coffee in the only café that would let them in. Witter sat with his drink in front of him, sipping when Sun did, mirroring him rather than drinking for enjoyment or refreshment. Sun found it fascinating and unsettling. This, he decided, was not the way he would end up. He was more clever than Witter and less greedy. He wanted neither riches nor the satisfaction of getting one over on the masters. They were off limits, too terrifying to have any contact with. He had used middlemen, or whatever the creatures from the darkworlds were, to take messages back and forth, to reveal his knowledge of The Association and their intentions. And all he wanted in return was safe passage from whatever chaos was likely to ensue.

That, and Yellow Jack.

Unknown on Earth, Yellow Jack was nevertheless a thorn in its side. Infused with every disease that had ever plagued the human race, he was Death itself to anyone he touched, but his taste for pleasure was even larger than his taste for Death. Sheathed and tethered he would be the lover Christopher Sun had always dreamed of. To the masters he was useful, but not indispensable. It was a good trade.

The venue for the meeting was a faceless room in a building tall enough to look down on those around it. How symbolic, thought Sun as he stepped out of the lift; *we are anonymous but so much More than you'll ever be.* They were met by a man who couldn't have been more than twenty years old, although he was doing his best to look older. He had to be an apprentice, thought Sun, a lackey, hoping to join the big boys of The Association. Sun almost told the boy to run, run as fast and as far as he could, while he could, but mercy would be seen as weakness, by either side, so he said nothing. The lackey took them to a door. He made to knock but stopped and turned.

"I just wanted to say, Mr Witter, that it's a privilege to meet you, Sir. The Association wouldn't exist without you. Your name is legendary."

A burst of laughter escaped Sun's lips. He immediately felt more confident about the meeting. The lackey opened the door and a group of middle-aged men stood up in reverent silence. Their expressions of respect and anticipation melted away as soon as they saw Witter. Two or three of them, old friends of his, Sun assumed, looked positively devastated. And why wouldn't they, Sun thought. Witter had been their ideal, the tough talking, ball-busting, no holds barred businessmen of their dreams. What stood before them was pitiful, a wreck that looked about to break into a thousand pieces.

One recovered himself quickly and thrust out a hand.

"Martin! It's been so long. Where have you been all this time? I had my money on Central America."

"I said Thailand," said another. "A man can choose not to be found in Thailand. And enjoy it, eh?"

Witter knew what was expected of him. He had been briefed on many things. He shuffled forward and took the man's hand.

"Here I am, Roger. Back again. But you've lost your money. You all have. I've been in the darkworlds. I've spent the last ten years in Hell."

And to their acute embarrassment, he began to cry.

It didn't last long and when it was over Sun could see that everyone had instantly erased The Moment from memory. A gray suit at the far end of the table opened the meeting.

"On behalf of everyone here, I'd like to say that it's good to have you back, Mr Witter. The Association was formed after you… left, by the friends you trusted enough to tell about the deal you were brokering. Our goal is simple—to continue in the vein of the job you began. It's taken us years to get this trusted band of men together," he gestured around the room, "and it seems there was a reason it took so long. You're back to oversee things. Give us your expert opinion."

Witter looked slowly around the table. "What is it, exactly, that you think you're going to do?" he said.

"That… country you mentioned; the darkworlds," said Roger. "You told me the place contained amazing properties," (and Sun could not help smirk at Roger's unintentional double meaning), "that if one were taken there at the point of Death, then Death itself could be cheated."

"It's true," said Witter. "But if there's one thing I've learned, it's this; why would anyone *want* to cheat Death?"

Tears began to stream from his eyes again. The lackey was sent to fetch water. The rest of the men looked at one another.

"We have a list of clients," said one.

"The rich. The super-rich," said another.

"All are eager to be interred, if that's the right word, in the darkworlds," said the gray suit. "And will pay us a colossal amount of money to make it happen."

"You'll have to disappoint your clients, then," said Witter. "None of you people have any business to be there."

Roger slammed his hand on the table. "These are not the sort of clients to disappoint!" he snarled.

"And the darkworlds are not a place to be bought and sold!"

For a moment Sun thought he had spoken the words, but Witter, standing up with spittle on his swollen lips, had made the statement.

"I must say," said an elderly man who had not spoken before, "that you're not living up to your reputation, Martin. I think we're all a little disappointed."

Sun grinned broadly. It seemed they had genuinely thought that this would be Martin Witter's grand return from exile, that he would do the final negotiations to give the richest humans on Earth the one thing they hadn't been able to buy. They evidently had no understanding of what eternity in the darkworlds would be like. Some, no doubt, would enjoy it, as Yellow Jack did, despite all the complaining

Sun had heard he was capable of, but most would spend Forever screaming for release.

Add to that the masters' fury at the proposed intrusion into their sacred space, the perpetuation of the arrogance they thought had crumbled as Witter had crumbled at their touch, and the twelve men and one boy around the table were, unless they were very lucky, utterly doomed.

Witter spoke again. "You've all seen what happened at the Tower of London. You must withdraw your plan. The masters demand it. I am not the man that some of you knew. The masters saw to that. If you want proof—"

He pulled his shirt up and uncovered his belly. The lackey was close by so Witter grabbed his hand and placed it on his stomach.

"Here's proof! Tell them, boy, how you can feel my heart beating in my bowels. They reconstructed me."

The lackey tried in vain to pull his hand away. He said nothing, but a retching sound came from his throat, and his expression was more joy for Sun to behold.

The Association was clearly in disarray. Confused and agitated, they proposed reconvening in a few days. Perhaps, thought Sun, they assumed Martin Witter would by then have become his old, greedy, ruthless self, a man without a heart. Which was preferable, after all, to having one that lay on a bed of one's own waste.

The dust had long since settled around the Tower of London, but the light streaming through the Keep's windows still showed a cloud rising slowly up from the inner chasm. The outside world was building makeshift bridges. It would soon find its way to the White Tower and attempt to find the bodies that lay far below the surface. The prying eyes had to be dissuaded and the cloud was there to dissuade them. It was made up of the smell and the taste and the feel of the darkworlds. It would clog the lungs and churn the stomach and cause the bowels to empty. It would penetrate masks and corrode oxygen tanks. The outside world could do whatever it wanted outside the White Tower; there were plenty of dead in the outer chasm to find, if they had the resources and the courage to look deep enough, but the White Tower belonged to the darkworlds. The ladders and steps were being put to good use, their lower levels swarming with natives of the darkworlds, fighting for the honour of going first. When the masters arrived order would be restored and the masses would begin to climb but for now it was chaotic. Much to the delight and terror of the participants.

Cara had gone home from the Tower of London and had meant to research the ravens but instead had fallen asleep. She woke up for long enough to get into bed and then fell back to sleep. She hoped not to dream but it was inevitable that she would, and she awoke with the taste of biscuits in her mouth. Biscuits and something else: blood.

Everything you dream is real.

Whoever the Eternal Traveller was, or had been. she was certainly capable of reading minds. Cara's dreams were the bane and the beauty of her life. Vivid to the point of super-reality, there was a time during her childhood where she couldn't distinguish between her dream-life and her waking-life. In her mid-teens she discovered that other cultures took dreams as seriously as she did. She was not alone, although when faced with the derision of a teacher she had felt completely isolated. "They're not real," he'd said, almost laughing. He'd slapped his hand on his desk. "This is real. And this!" He'd smacked the blackboard, smiling as the rest of the class jeered. Since then she'd been careful who she talked to, who she trusted. She'd bumped around the fringes of paranormal groups, psychics, dowsers, finding pockets of hokum but also great expanses of truth. She'd never been perceived by these people as someone with any great power or gift. She considered herself more of an observer than a participant. So why did the Eternal Traveller think she was worthy of contact, that she would be able to comprehend what was happening and could even change the outcome?

It had to be the dreams. Although tonight's offerings, great flocks of ravens, each one completely indistinguishable from the rest, followed by great flocks of the repulsive Things that had dropped the two men onto the street, gave no insights. She couldn't remember any dreams that had foreseen future events or had any practical use. They were just different lives on different worlds.

And could the threat of the darkworlds by extinguished by the simple yet almost impossible act of finding a raven? She knew virtually nothing about the birds. How far from the Tower would they have flown? How could any of them be identified? And if she failed, what then?

The whole world shall fall if the chasm remains.

These were the words of the Eternal Traveller and she knew what they meant; the apocalyptic wasteland of her worst nightmares, the brilliant but terrifying super-structures that she'd dreamt of, the architecture of the darkworlds elevated to the surface of the Earth.

Despite herself, she slept again.

The Eternal Traveller had watched Cara sleep. Her original idea had been to take Cara on a secret visit to the darkworlds so she'd have no doubt as to what they were up against, but that would have meant Cara being in a state of near death. There was no place in the darkworlds for the living, even on a brief visit. It was too risky, the Eternal Traveller had decided. Cara Limehouse needed to be alive when she took one of the Tower's ravens back home. Then the curse would be broken and the darkworlds would be sealed off. Not destroyed (she did not know if it could be destroyed) but kept at bay, away from the living things on Earth. Most of them, anyway. No. The Eternal Traveller would have to go alone.

She could feel the dreadful energy of the ranks massing far below the White Tower. Time was of the essence; the outer chasm would be quiet. This was where the vast majority of the dead lay. Most would have been crushed or smashed to pieces. Some, she knew, would have been taken for an eternal half-life into the darkworlds. She hoped to find the Ravenmaster hiding among the peaceful dead. He'd loved, fed and cared for the birds for many years. He would know where they were likely to have gone and how to bring at least one of them back.

The Eternal Traveller threw off the near-human shape she'd taken on and floated out of Cara's open window. She made her way along the streets, still quiet in the breaking day, enjoying the city she'd spent her whole life in, tempted to visit friends and relatives but knowing that now was not the time. Her spirit—one moment the shape of a bird, the next a double-helix, the next a chaosphere—reached the Tower unnoticed, the few people it passed plugged in to their own defences against the city and unaware of the dead soul in their midst. Not wanting to scare the Ravenmaster, she took on her human form again but as she tumbled into the outer chasm she realised she was not alone.

Cara Limehouse's dream-self was with her.

In the hours since the chaotic end to the meeting with The Association, all sixty-four and three-quarters of them, Sun realised he had still not got the measure of Martin Witter. The man-wreckage he had scorned on sight had an iron will and the strength of a dozen ordinary people. Of course, he was acting on the instructions of the masters, with the threat of some hellish retribution should he falter, but Witter was nevertheless in dire physical and mental agony. A little respect was deserved. Witter did not need to be a stinking mess for The Association to see what the masters could do. Sun took him home and scrubbed him clean. The act of kindness was one Sun declared he'd never repeat; naked, the full extent of Witter's rebuilding was obvious. Bones, clearly in the wrong place, slipped in and out of joints. The cartilage that remained was not enough to keep them secure and so bones pushed up under skin, threatening to tear it. Sun finished as quickly as he could and dressed him in the best suit he had, knowing all the while how pointless the gesture was in making Witter more comfortable.

They sat in the same dreary office the previous meeting had taken place in. Sun had managed to wring smatterings of conversation from Witter; memories of his son, his life before the darkworlds and his insane intention to detonate a biological weapon in the place. Sun had asked him repeatedly about Yellow Jack but Witter had said virtually nothing. It was clear the two detested each other and Sun had heard hints of a dalliance of sorts between Jack and the young man, Boyd. And while Witter had not changed his politics of wild bigotry, his perspective on what made the world turn was altered beyond all recognition of those who had known him. Witter had been educated and realised now that the masters were more powerful than money, land, property... all the things he had worshipped. They were probably more powerful than God, but on that Witter was silent, presumably hoping that God would still be around when the masters had no further use for him.

This change became obvious when The Association trooped in, take-away coffees in hand, and sat down. Their first question, naturally, was why Witter had insisted on such an early hour for the meeting. In reply, Witter looked at the clock on the wall.

"It's 4– 48 am," he said. "The exact time that most suicides kill themselves. You people are determined to die. Therefore the time is appropriate."

The Association members simply looked at one another, wide-eyed. Sun noted this had been their response to most of what Witter said. They were clearly not taking him seriously, not believing what their eyes saw.

"Okay, Martin, dramatic point made," said Roger, toasting him with his coffee cup. "We still plan to make us all unimaginably wealthy. You're included in that plan, if you help us. We know you can help us, that you can be the go-between that makes this all work smoothly. All you have to do is say yes."

"It's clear you've had a rough time of it, that you're not well," piped up a man who hadn't spoken before. Sun looked at him properly for the first time and was struck by a certainty that the man had begun life as biologically female. Sun wondered if the others knew their colleague was transgendered. Would they care? After all, surely the ability to trample upon others and make money was what counted, not one's gender.

"We can get you the best medical care," he continued. "For whatever's wrong…"

Sun was tiring of it all. The Association, powerful as they were, were fools. Of all of them only the lackey had the intelligence to look fearful. And Sun, happy to be unacknowledged during the initial meeting when he was sure Witter's appearance would be enough to convince them, was tired of being invisible. He tightened his hand to a fist and banged the table like a Judge bringing a court to order.

"Are you too stupid to understand what Witter's saying? Or is it just too inconvenient to accept?" he said. "Look at him. What the masters did to him terrifies me and it should terrify you. They will not let you exploit the darkworlds. They don't give a fuck how rich your clients are. Stop now or the whole world will suffer. And pray it's not too late."

"And who are you? Are you from the darkworlds?" asked Roger.

"My name is Christopher Sun. I'm not from the darkworlds, but I know enough about them to know you haven't got a hope. You cannot succeed. I'm trying to save your fucking lives, and the lives of your families, your grandchildren."

The gray suited man spoke up. "The Association has dealt with surly natives before. The Association is made of stern stuff. If you cannot join us, Mr Witter, it will delay things a little. And it would be a shame not to have you with us. But we are determined to continue and I would hope that neither of you are foolish enough to attempt to stand in our way."

The meeting was over. It had lasted barely forty minutes. Witter was shaking, desperate at his failure. Sun took his arm, guiding him out of the building and towards a road where they'd find a cab. What next? Take Witter back to his flat to rest, report to the masters, and hope they kept their side of the bargain. Sun shivered at the thought of what the world would become after the masters took their revenge. He heard footsteps behind him and turned to find the transgendered Association member behind them.

"We weren't properly introduced," he said. "My name is James Dodd. I know Mr Witter only by reputation, and it is quite some reputation. If being in the darkworlds has had this affect on you, sir, then it must be a formidable place and I think we should know exactly what it is we're taking on."

One of The Association, at least, had been listening.

"Have you been to the Tower of London since the so-called disaster?" asked Sun.

Dodd shook his head. "I thought it was an earthquake. It didn't occur to me to connect it to the darkworlds."

"Or, more accurately, your plan for the darkworlds," said Sun. "The fact that you never even considered it just proves your arrogance. There's an awful lot of blood on your hands, Dodd."

"There was long before this," replied Dodd grimly. "The Association has its sources; we've mapped fragments of the darkworlds," he didn't add that the maps didn't make sense, that its contours and features contradicted themselves, "but it's still such unknown territory. Martin, could you describe the place to me, in a way I can understand?"

Witter met Dodd's eyes, hoping that one gaze would be enough, would describe everything without the need for words. He thought of the fissure, crammed with the should-be dead; humans, animals, insects, all pushing, fighting, biting for space, for the illusion of air, the blood and pus and bile that covered the walls making them impossible to climb. He thought of the hills he'd ascended, thinking he could escape, then breathlessly reaching the top and finding only the endless landscape he'd begun in. He thought of the fields covered in blood and craters like a First World War battlefield, with the remains of men and women stumbling along, looking for somewhere quiet to hide and be left alone.

And he thought of those who were worst of all; the ones who looked as if they'd found the Promised Land. The ones who felt at home.

James Dodd had, it appeared, taken much of it in. He seemed hypnotised by it. He muttered something which neither Sun nor Witter could hear. He repeated it.

"How do you keep the dragons away in such a place?"

Then he gestured with his arms, waving them above his head. "A therapist once told me this," he said. "'There was a man in the street, waving his arms around. I went up to him and asked him why he was doing it. The man told me that as long as he waved, the dragons would keep away. I told him that there were no dragons and he replied, *Exactly*.'"

Witter, aware of movement growing in the

shadows, gave Dodd a sad look. "Whether you wave your arms or not, I assure you, the dragons will come anyway."

He took Sun's arm for support and they walked away. There was the sound of a scuffle behind them, followed by a scream cut short to a death rattle. Sun resisted the temptation to look back.

Had he done so, he would have been delighted to come face to face with Yellow Jack.

"What you will see here," said the Eternal Traveller to Cara, "is the result of death in extraordinary circumstances. Do not let what you will see here frighten you off death."

The species of the dead, she explained, *are as many and varied as the species of the living. There are those that are content with their being, now free of the bodies that held them to the world. There are the ghosts, the ones who are not able to let go of the life that has gone. There are those who have been carried off to the further reaches of limbo, such as those who find themselves in the darkworlds. And there are the unhappy souls who, completely unprepared, find themselves dead and have no comprehension of what has happened.*

Edward Gill was one of the unhappy souls, the Eternal Traveller realised as soon as she saw his body. The soul that had been the Ravenmaster was hiding in the smashed remains of his corpse, some of which had been flattened under rock and earth. Pieces of other bodies and lumps of flesh and bone lay around him. The Eternal Traveller could only imagine how terrifying it would have been for him to awake to.

Cara was also struggling. Her physical body, safe in bed at home, was whimpering at the dreadful dream-scene. At the bottom of the outer chasm, the Eternal Traveller put a reassuring hand on Cara's arm.

"We are in such luck, Cara!" she said. "The Ravenmaster could have been taken to the darkworlds, or his spirit could have been crossing the Universe, but he's here, still in his body."

Cara shuddered, wondering how any part of a person could survive in such remains. Much of Edward Gill's face had been destroyed but one eye and his jaw was intact. The Eternal Traveller crouched down and brushed the mud off what was left of his cheek.

"Edward? Speak to me, Ravenmaster. The living need you."

His one eye moved to look at her. The light that had gone from it days before returned and his jaw inched open. A sound, not unlike the whimpering Cara was making in her bed, came from his mouth before he managed to speak.

"Be quiet! Or the Devil will come back for me. He's taken some of the others already. They were so wounded but He made them get up and He led them away..."

The whimpering returned. The Eternal Traveller held up her hand. "You're safe. You've been dead for too long for those devils to get you. I can set your soul free but I need to find your ravens and take them home."

The Ravenmaster gave a sigh. "My beautiful ravens are dead."

"That's not true. They flew away before the disaster. They all left the Tower's grounds. They're alive, Edward, and I must find them."

"They're alive? That's wonderful. But if they all left then the curse must have been real."

Cara knelt beside Gill's body and spoke to him.

"We don't know for sure. But we need to find your ravens and make sure they're safe. Where would they go? How can we identify them?

"Each has a coloured band around its leg. Some have flown away before. I found them in the East End. James Crow, he's the oldest, is likely to be at a pub begging for beer. The others are named George, Grog, Edgar Sopper, Charlie, Rhys, and Mabel. They all answer to their names. Be kind to them."

The Eternal Traveller shook Gill's soul free. Cara gasped as the sphere of brilliant orange light appeared from Gill's broken corpse. Liberated, it shot up and away from the darkworlds, out of the outer chasm and towards the sky.

"There goes a contented soul," said the Eternal Traveller. "As now you must go, Cara, back to your body. I'm glad you were here, but it's too dangerous for you to continue. When you wake up, you'll know what you have to do."

And as Cara faded from view, the Eternal Traveller turned and headed further into the darkworlds.

Once away from the rubble and the bodies, the Eternal Traveller found herself in the foothills of the darkworlds. It was an extraordinary place, a humid forest of rotting vegetation. Gigantic flies and mosquitoes bumped past her but, having no blood to steal, none of the insects had any interest in her. There were strange buildings amongst the plants. All had succumbed to the vegetation. Ahead of her rose a mountain, arid and bare, steam rising from its rocks. Halfway up she could clearly see the temples that had been built.

Were they sanctuary for the poor souls here or places of worship for them to appease the masters?

Could such creatures *be* appeased?

She realised she was being watched. A wraith-like young man with a repulsive dog at his side got up from the plant he'd been sitting against and made his way over. The young man had lumps of stinking vegetation in his hair and the dog was covered in a moving coat of lice.

"You're not like the rest of us," he said. "People sometimes come from the outside, those who don't know how lucky they are, usually. Are you a tourist?"

The Eternal Traveller gave a wry laugh. "No, lad. I'd rather not be here at all. But I'm not like those on the outside, either. I just needed to see what this place was really like. To keep me focussed. How long have you been here?"

"I was born here," said the youth. "I found Sobersides. We look after each other."

Sobersides looked barely able to stand up, thought the Eternal Traveller, much less protect its companion.

"Have you ever seen the masters?" she asked.

The youth's eyes widened. "I hear them sometimes. The sounds they make bounce off the trees and form horrible shapes. I stay in the forest with Sobersides. The insects bite all the time but it's safer here. It's safer everywhere now; most of the others are going up to the surface."

An invasion! The Eternal Traveller had feared as much. She asked the youth where the exodus was beginning from and he pointed towards the foot of the mountain.

"There's a hole in the sky. They all want to be first out. You'll hear them fighting for the ladders before you see them."

It looked a huge distance away but the Eternal Traveller found herself there in minutes. No senses were to be trusted here. As the youth had predicted, she heard the fracas before she saw who was making it. Yowling, howling, threats, growls, and the sounds of fighting reached her before she was halfway there. And then she saw the hole in the sky; a long rectangle in the clouds. A single stone stairway led up to it but the darkworlds' citizens had made a number of ladders that stretched into the hole. Each ladder was heaving with shapes that fought for position. Some of the fighting was good natured but most of it was vicious.

And one of the creatures was wearing a Beefeater's coat. Whether it had been stolen from a corpse or whether the Beefeater had been unfortunate enough to survive the fall was impossible to tell. The thing wearing the coat had a man's shape, but its bearing and the sounds it made were those of a lost soul. But still it fought to climb further up one of the ladders and the movement above confirmed what the Eternal Traveller most feared; that the inhabitants of the darkworlds meant to wrest a terrible revenge for the misdemeanours of The Association.

She had seen enough. The quickest way out would be to soar up the inner chasm, but she was bound to be seen, so she returned the way she had come. On her way back through the forest she spied Sobersides looking, if it were possible, even more morose than it had done before.

The youth was lying on the ground, face up, eyes staring skyward. At first the Eternal Traveller thought he was alive but then she was relieved that he was not; fungus, long, thin and white like a lamprey, had curled its way up from the ground, through his torso and out of his stomach, killing him as he had lay down to rest. In that moment she realised the true ideology of the darkworlds. It was not horror, or fear, or brutality, although it revelled in all of these things.

What was really sacred to this place was sadness.

If the Eternal Traveller had spoken to Martin Witter, he would have been able to tell her all about sadness, and anguish with it. When he'd been alive he had refused to acknowledge such feelings, and those parts of his brain had all but shut down, but when the masters had him they had known what would hurt him most and had left his brain, and conscience, in a better state than it had been before. He was thus able to appreciate the physical agony of his badly reassembled body and the mental pain of all he had done, or not done in his life. While he was in no doubt of the foolishness of his desire to sell off the darkworlds as if it was a charming coastal home, he had been utterly devastated by the way he had treated Boyd, his only child. Boyd's life, dressing in girls' clothes, refusing to fight or do anything normal boys did, and then experimenting with drugs and magic, had been an embarrassment and his death, in some bizarre ritual in a filthy squat, a further inconvenience. In truth he had been unable to feel anything else, but the masters had changed all that and he'd spent the last ten years burning with grief and guilt. Stumbling around the darkworlds, he had been moved to painful tears by the condition of its citizens, something that would have been impossible during his lifetime.

But even the masters had been unable to switch off his loathing of his son's ugly, diseased lover Yellow Jack, and when Christopher Sun opened the door of his flat to find Jack standing there, Witter vomited. Of course Sun, after a moment of panic, realised who had come to visit and was as excited as a child at Christmas.

Witter's first impression of Sun as a fool had not changed. Yellow Jack, who Witter had managed to avoid in the darkworlds, strode into Sun's home and assumed control.

"I've been following you from the City," he said. "I thought you might at least have watched me deal with that Association filth."

"That was you?" said Sun. "James Dodd was thinking of changing sides. He was unsettled at the meeting and once Witter had told him what he was taking on he was wavering. We might have been able to use him..." he trailed off, not wanting to criticise either Yellow Jack or the masters' tactics.

"They've had years to come to their senses," said Jack. "It's too late. Some of The Association will live long enough to see the destruction their arrogance has caused. Then they'll be destroyed, along with hundreds of thousands of others. The Tower of London is crawling with our people. They'll spread through the country like a disease." He smiled.

"Is the Torquis with them?" asked Witter. In all his years in the darkworlds he had not come across his son's killer. If she was taking part in the retribution, he would tear her apart and damn the consequences.

Yellow Jack, the smile still on his face, slowly shook his head. "The Torquis is long dead. The masters reward their most faithful. She wanted peace and she has it. When are you going to accept that Boyd went looking for death, or something resembling it, long before he met her? Neither of us is to blame for your son's peccadillos."

That silenced Witter. Jack turned his attention to Christopher Sun.

"You were there when the Tower fell. What happened?"

Sun told him about the legend of the Tower's ravens, how he had used them, timed to perfection, to make the legend appear real. To his disappointment, Jack was not particularly impressed.

"Did anyone, or any *thing*, try to stop you?" he asked.

"No. Apart from a couple of police officers and Beefeaters; they just ran into the chasm. It was chaos. No one knew what was going on."

"What about the ravens? Were they killed?"

Sun shrugged. "As far as I know, they flew away. What does it matter?"

Jack glared at him. "Everything matters. There are rumours of opposition to the invasion. They say something's travelled most of the Universe to seal the darkworlds back up. It's not just The Association we're dealing with."

Sun clearly had no idea what Jack was talking about, but tried to bullshit his way through.

"Nothing can stop the reprisal! Or The Association will regain momentum." Sun opened his laptop and searched the Holy of Holies; the Internet. From the corner of his eye, he watched as Jack took off his gloves, picked out a cd, caressed it, then replaced his gloves. The threat was more than implied, but still a thrill ran down Sun's spine.

"There are a million references to the Tower's collapse," he said. He looked through half a dozen pages then re-wrote the search terms. And it was there.

"This could be interesting, " he said as casually as he could. "It's a conversation on an Earth Energies forum."

He clicked on the page, then ran a programme that unlocked all the forum's private messages. Most were irrelevant so he erased them. What were left were the conversations between Spyglass, the Eternal Traveller, and Sasquatch.

"Spyglass is definitely writing from London but Eternal Traveller is from a very weird source. I can't trace it," he said, aware that Jack was right behind him now, reading what little there was.

"It's enough to make it worth tracking them down," said Jack. "Or perhaps I'll start with the ravens. Wiping them out could be vital."

"It's only a story," said Sun, his tone more mocking than he had intended. Jack ignored him and made to leave, so Sun got up from his desk, passed the silent, dejected form of Martin Witter and opened the door.

"You'll be hearing from me," said Jack. "Set up another meeting with The Association. String them along a bit. And see how depleted their numbers are getting." He turned back in the hallway. "Oh, and there's no such thing as 'only stories'; everything comes from somewhere."

Sun went back inside and returned the cd to his collection. There was never any excuse for untidiness.

The White Tower had been subject to a curious attack. Its entrances had been wrapped in a biohazard tent after half a dozen soldiers had died appalling deaths while trying to investigate the inner chasm. The tent had been extended to the building's windows which had all been smashed, from the inside, long after the soldiers had staggered out, drooling blood.

Violent deaths began to occur in London. Not in itself unusual, but the manner of them—grotesque, bizarre, freakish—shocked the officers who dealt with them. And the locations: one or two were in gangland inner city slums and tower blocks, but most were in gentrified areas and the suburbs before spreading out to the Home Counties. One woman in Hornchurch died of what appeared to be the Bubonic Plague. A man was decapitated, his head impaled on a spiked railing in a beautiful Georgian square in Islington. And what's more, *strange individuals* were reported all over the capital. Not the mad or the intoxicated that are part of any city's make-up, but others who either looked or behaved so oddly they frightened even the hardiest Londoner. Soon enough, the whole of Greater London was living in fear.

The reprisal had begun.

The Association had lost two further members since James Dodd's terrible end, whose post-mortem had revealed surprisingly more than his cause of death. In the true spirit of stubbornness and arrogance, however, The Association was determined to continue. Clients were reassured, contracts drawn up, mercenaries hired to physically clear the darkworlds, if necessary, of surly natives.

Cara Limehouse had woken from the darkworlds dream, reached for her pen and dream diary and scribbled down as much as she could remember. Even before she'd checked her phone and realised that she'd spent nearly two days asleep, she knew the dream had been as real as any waking experience she'd ever had. She remembered the ravens' names and where they might be and then she remembered the Ravenmaster's soul freed from his remains, and she cried with happiness, wonder, and fright. Later, after she'd showered and fed herself, she wondered if she would see the Eternal Traveller again. She had the distinct feeling she would be searching for the ravens alone.

After printing off details of all the pubs around

the Tower and the East End, she grabbed her London A-Z, some biscuits to tempt the ravens with, and a large, black cloth to capture them in.

The logical place to begin was close to the Tower so she took a bus to the Traitor's Arms. It was a nondescript place, catering for tourists rather than locals and she felt sure the birds would not be here. The next nearest pubs were just over the river, so she quickly crossed Tower Bridge, turned down a dark, ancient looking passageway, and found the next pub. No ravens were there, or had been spotted according to the landlady, so she walked on.

As she entered The Three Remarkable Steeples the hairs on the back of her neck stood up. The pub was full. But not of drinkers; the place was crowded with ghosts, the most blatant haunting she'd ever experienced. She ordered a half pint of beer and asked the barmaid about the pub's odd name.

"It's named after a building that stood on this site in medieval times. It looked like a church but had three steeples that leant at angles as if they were falling. There's a picture of it in the toilets."

Of course, thought Cara. A building's history, folklore, architecture, good only to while away the queue for a piss. She asked if the beer garden was open.

"It is, dear, but be careful. We've had a few crows around trying to steal beer, the cheeky buggers."

The beer garden was more of a yard, with a couple of picnic tables on one side and beer barrels on the other. In a corner stood a small aviary. Cara put her drink on a table and went over to it. She'd always hated caged animals. The birds here seemed content but the place for them was the open skies, not this prison. The sound of fluttering wings behind her made her turn, carefully, and there, eyeing her drink, was a raven. She had never realised quite how big such a bird was. How anyone could mistake it for a crow was beyond her. As it strutted across the table she noticed a red band around one of its legs.

This was one of the Tower's ravens.

"Are you James Crow? The Ravenmaster said you liked a drink."

The raven took a beakful of beer.

"Charlie? Mabel?" Cara reeled off the names the Ravenmaster had given them. There was a second fluttering of wings behind her. Two ravens were better than one. She turned around, a smile on her face and met the grimace of a decomposing, winged horse. It stared at her through eyeless sockets, its wings aloft as it landed on the concrete of the yard. Lumps of flesh swung from its bones. A piece splattered to the ground when flicked by its swishing tail.

So this was what a creature of the darkworlds looked like, close up. She had seen mercifully little before, outside the Tower with the Eternal Traveller. As her nerves began to fail, the clunk of glass against wood reassured her. The raven was still there. If she could only win its trust. She reached into her rucksack and picked out a biscuit.

"Grog? Come to me, Grog."

The man talking to the raven was behind the horse. At least, it was a version of a man. Yellow Jack, splattered with filth and blood, had the air of a weary, dehumanised soldier.

"What did you think one of the horsemen of the apocalypse would wear?" he said. "A nice, shiny suit of armour?"

"You're from the darkworlds," said Cara.

Yellow Jack gave a short bow. "And you've

crossed the Universe to be here?"

So he knew of the Eternal Traveller. Should she pretend to be her? Would it be better or worse for her?

"I know the raven's name and I have its favourite food," Jack continued. "It will come to me and I'll tear it in half."

"I only need to take one raven back to the Tower," said Cara. "I'll find the others."

"And I'll tear *them* in two," said Jack. "And then I'll let War," he gestured towards the horse, "have you. She does love human meat. And that's all you are, isn't it?"

He pulled a handkerchief from his pocket and lay it on the furthest table. Inside was a mound of broken biscuits. From another pocket he took a second handkerchief, heavy and sodden with a dark liquid. He wrung it over the biscuits and thick blood oozed down onto them.

Biscuits and blood. Cara had dreamt of them, had awoken with their taste in her mouth, but had failed to understand their significance.

Everything you dream is real.

"Come to me, Grog," said Yellow Jack again.

The raven looked up from its beer, attracted by the smell of blood and the man calling its name. Then it flew to the blood soaked biscuits and Yellow Jack smiled.

The hapless remains of The Association sat around the table. Not in the office high above the City of London; this time they were meeting in a room above a pub. It was quiet and dark; they felt a little safer here, although none would admit to being terrified. Nearly half their number was dead. The remaining members, eyes darkened from lack of sleep, sank back in their seats, whiskies in hand, waiting for Martin Witter and his slimy friend to arrive and put an end to the nightmare.

But still there was the thought; less members means even more money for the rest of us. If Witter could only calm things down, the plan could still be put into operation. There'd be enough money to buy the remaining Association members and their families a ticket into space. Even the masters and their very surly natives couldn't follow them there. Could they?

They recognised the painful shuffle of Martin Witter as soon as he appeared, with the slimy friend in tow.

Christopher Sun had large drinks for both of them. After all, they were here to gloat, to celebrate. and took a mouthful as soon as they sat down. The Association's arrogance was waning, he noted. Perhaps today would be the day they'd realise how key Christopher Sun had been to the collapse of their life's work.

"Well, now," he said, enjoying the moment. "Are there enough of you here? Is this meeting quorate?"

Six pairs of eyes, seven including the trembling lackey, stared at him. Roger was present, but only in body. His spirit seemed to have deserted him. He spoke at last.

"Everything you warned us about is happening. We were stupid to think we could go through with the plan. For God's sake, Martin, call off the dogs."

Witter poured the whisky down his throat in one go, force of habit from the old days, and gasped for air. When he'd recovered, he responded.

"It's not that easy. I'll return to the darkworlds as soon as I can, but I don't have any say in what happens. You can but hope."

To everyone's surprise the lackey had something to say.

"Please. You must be able to stop this. The way the others died... There are madmen on the streets. It's spreading out from London. I don't want to die!"

The others murmured, no doubt privately in agreement, but publicly despising the lackey's display of honesty.

"You don't want to die? That can be arranged," said Sun. He beckoned at the shadows.

The woman who stepped out was dressed in a style that had been fashionable a century or more ago. Her dress, once of the finest quality, was now threadbare, with moths and insects clinging to the remains. The woman smiled with difficulty, her face having at some point been removed and another, ill fitting around her skull and nose, stitched clumsily on. A woodlouse fell from her mouth.

"This is Catherine Xos. She'll take you to the darkworlds," said Sun. "Be happy. You're leaving all this madness behind."

The woman closed a frozen hand around the lackey's arm, so tight the bone fractured. He mewled in pain and fear and begged his fellow Association members to help him. They stared blankly ahead. He was not yet truly one of them, was still working his way into the true circle of The Association. He was not worth dying for.

And if the plan somehow went ahead, it would mean more money for the rest of them.

Sun beamed as the lackey, now quiet, was led away, while Martin Witter let out a sob. He alone knew what might await the boy. Furthermore, the lad was someone's child. His parents would soon realise he was missing.

Sun finished his drink. "I think that concludes the meeting. The Association will destroy any papers, computer files, and any thoughts of desecrating the darkworlds. Mr Witter will confirm this to the masters. And we'll see if the merry chaos subsides. The new merry chaos, that is. The usual chaos will continue, I dare say."

He turned once as he headed towards the stairs, taking in the bowed heads, the fragrance of terror. Every detail mattered. The masters might require evidence of complete success. And he was quite happy to be parting company from Martin Witter. The man was too frightening a reminder of what the masters could do. And very poor company to boot.

"I assume you're going to the Tower of London now?" he wanted confirmation.

Witter shuddered. "Yes, I must. *Something* will be there to take me to the staircase at the inner chasm."

"If you're lucky, if the masters are happy, they might let you die. Me, I'll batten down the hatches at home and await my reward."

Witter almost laughed then. "Your reward? Are you sure about that?"

"I've been promised Yellow Jack. Bound and tethered, you might like to hear, to do with as I please."

"I hope you have time to enjoy him. Or have you forgotten the compact disc he touched that you so thoughtlessly picked up and put away?"

Witter waited, watching the incomprehension on Sun's face, then the remembering, and with the remembering the realisation that he was done for. What little was left of the old Martin Witter drank it in. It was all he would have for company on the agonising walk back down the staircase to the darkworlds, a journey that might last a thousand years.

Grog was enjoying the bloody biscuits. Yellow Jack let it feed. He wanted to squeeze as much enjoyment out of winning as possible. For Cara, time seemed to have stopped. She could not afford to assume she'd get to any of the other ravens first, or even that she'd find them. She had to get Grog to the Tower.

Outnumbered, a diversion was her only hope. She stole a quick glance around the yard and saw the aviary. She turned and ran to it, flicked the catch on the door and opened it, then stepped inside and waved the panicking birds to freedom. The yard was instantly full of finches and budgies and the skeleton horse, excited at the sight of food flying around her, jumped up and began snapping at the birds. To Cara's horror, she bit one in half and swallowed another two whole, then rose up and flew around the yard.

Yellow Jack roared at her to come down. He took a step away from Grog, who was still eating, and Cara knew this would be her only chance. She crossed the yard and threw the cloth over Grog in one movement. Scooping the raven up, she ran through the pub and out the front door, zig-zagging through the back streets, onto the main road, onto a bus that was heading back across the river to the Tower of London.

The journey, barely a mile, was the longest, most terrifying of Cara's life. Yellow Jack ran in the road beside the bus, punching at the doors and anything else he could reach. The bus driver took one look at him and accelerated. War flew along the other side of the bus. There was a *thump* as she landed briefly on the roof, then she slid off and began flying again.

Everyone except Cara was screaming. A teenage boy tried filming the horse on his phone, then thought better of it and cried for his mother instead. War was truly a terrible sight, made worse by the normality of everything around her. Pieces of horseflesh dropped onto cars and pedestrians as she veered back and forth and she kicked out at anything in her path. Grog had pecked at Cara for a while but the dark cloth soon quietened him down, much to her relief.

And the bus was out-running Yellow Jack.

If Cara was lucky, she would have time to run across to the Tower, climb over the barrier and release Grog before her pursuers caught up with her. And then, of course, pray that the Eternal Traveller had been right and that sanity would be restored. That was, until Yellow Jack and War got hold of her. Which might not be the case if the Eternal Traveller hadn't abandoned her, Cara thought bitterly.

But there was no time for self-pity. In an act so banal it was almost comical, Cara rang the bell and the bus stopped, with the Tower of London in full view just yards away. She got off, her precious bundle heavy in her arms, and prepared to save or lose the Kingdom.

The ruins of the Tower of London were guarded, but not heavily. It seemed that the continuing speculation as to the cause of the disaster and reports of ghosts of the victims roaming the area had scared sightseers away. The police were busy trying to solve the multiple, seemingly random murders that had been committed around the capital and beyond, so it had been left to a private, and therefore lax, security firm to keep an eye on the Tower until the authorities worked out what to do with it.

The closer Martin Witter got to the Tower, the more severe his pain became. His bones had broken away at the joints and his heart thumped around his bowels in constant palpitations. Worst of all, his grief for Boyd was increasing, the void of time not healing but yawning wider and emptier with every moment. The last thing he wanted to do was return to the darkworlds, but he knew it would be worse for him if he did not. He saw a guard doing his rounds and walked as casually as he could past him. His path took him alongside the river and towards Tower Bridge and there, not fifty yards away, was Yellow Jack. He was bent double, catching his breath.

He would never have a better chance for revenge.

Pieces of rubble that had been rescued from the edge of the outer chasm were still laid on the ground and Witter found a huge lump of masonry amongst it. When he picked it up he felt as if his body would burst with pain, but he persevered. Out of Jack's line of vision, he staggered closer. If he managed to kill Jack, or at least badly damage him, it would not only avenge Boyd, but would also spoil Christopher Sun's revolting plans, for as long as Sun lived, anyway. And that had to be worth the suffering.

Jack heard him, of course, as he made his final approach and managed to stand up and raise his arms.

"No! You don't understand, she has a raven!" he shouted and Witter realised the importance of it, but not soon enough to stop the masonry smashing Yellow Jack's skull.

Witter turned just in time to see a figure scrabbling over the barrier and under the biohazard tent. Yellow Jack was not, or had not been, one to be frivolous about the darkworlds and so Witter knew he'd have to kill the raven before he could return. He shuffled to the barrier and as he pulled himself up he heard the sound of heavy wings flapping. He looked up and his eyes met the disgusting sight of a maggoty, dead horse flying over the wall of the Tower.

Cara crawled out from under the fabric sheet and found herself inches away from the outer chasm. The memory of her dream-journey returned and she felt dizzy, but she pulled the bundle clear of the sheet. Scrabbling for the opening, she was about to release Grog when a lump of stinking flesh dropped to the ground beside her. War had arrived. Her other pursuer would be close behind. But War wasn't going to wait for him. The horse bent its skeleton neck and snapped at Cara's hand, breaking two of her fingers. Cara screamed as blood poured down her hand. War grabbed the cloth with her teeth and rose into the air with it. Grog was still alive, Cara was sure, but wouldn't be for long.

War rose higher and higher and was about to fly away from the Tower's grounds when a ball of light appeared from the top of the White Tower. Crackling with energy, it spun through the air like a Catherine Wheel and hit War in her bare ribs with tremendous force. The horse exploded, bones and flesh spraying in all directions. Grog tumbled out of its cloth prison and, free at last, flapped its wings and flew.

Cara cheered. The Eternal Traveller had not abandoned her after all. But Grog was airborne and could fly anywhere; her other pursuer was seconds away. And others from the darkworlds abounded; already a hideous face was peering at her from a shredded piece of sheeting around the White Tower. How could she bring Grog down? All she had was herself.

All she had was the blood on her hand.

Grog was still circling. She shouted for the bird

to come to her and held her throbbing, injured hand to the sky. And Grog, smelling blood, flew down in a neat spiral and landed at Cara's feet.

The effect was immediate. The ground began to shake, at first around Cara and Grog then spreading along the earth to the outer chasm, and then across the chasm to the White Tower. Cara crouched down and held her undamaged hand over the void. The air rippled around it. She shook some drops of blood onto the grass to keep Grog there, her eyes fixed on the chasm.

A skin was forming across it. The edges blurred, the vibrating air now lying flat and solidifying. The face that had been staring from the White Tower promptly disappeared; being trapped on the surface was unthinkable. Cara didn't notice. She was standing on the outer chasm, staring down at nothingness that was fast disappearing.

This was the sight that greeted Martin Witter as he crawled out from under the tent; Cara appearing to levitate. Above him was the sound of ravens clicking and rattling at one another as a flock of them gathered over the Tower of London.

Amongst them were the rest of the Tower's precious birds.

Witter was beside himself. He could blame the failure of the full invasion on Yellow Jack. But returning to the darkworlds and reporting to the masters was his responsibility alone. He stumbled across the outer chasm, desperately hoping to fall into it, then heaved his unnatural body up the wooden staircase, through the biohazard tent that had been effortlessly clawed into strips and to the inner chasm.

It was still there.

He loped around the edge of it, towards

the corner where the stone staircase fell away into darkness, but even as he made his pathetic way along he could see the skin forming over the chasm, so he dropped over the side and hoped to break through it.

And break through it he did; half way. He felt himself move though the thickening air but then he stopped. He was lying flat, face down, one arm above him and one below.

The air solidified around him. It became earth and stone. As the outside returned to what it had been before, one half of Martin Witter lay exposed in the serene surroundings of St John's Chapel. The other half faced the chasm, staring towards the darkworlds, a place he would never reach.

Witter took as much air into his crushed lungs as he could and tried to scream.

Buildings were rebuilding themselves, bricks and mortar flying through the air to their allotted places. It was not a safe place to be. Cara pushed the sheeting aside and fled, leaving an open-mouthed security guard in her wake. She ran to the Thames, to the place where she had seen the Eternal Traveller emerge and the ball of light was there in the shape of the strange woman who had saved her life. Cara tried to thank her but all she could do was cry.

"Don't thank me, Cara," said the Eternal Traveller. "You did most of the work. I just made a show of myself at the end." She was smiling.

"Is it over?" asked Cara.

"Yes and no. The darkworlds have been sealed and for that the masters might be furious but it appears the plan to exploit parts of it—and believe me, people would buy shares in Hell if they thought there was something in it for them, has been... deferred. Indefinitely."

"So that might satisfy the masters?"

"I hope it will. And who knows how many citizens of the darkworlds are still amok here in London or elsewhere? They'll like that. But it does mean it's not over."

Word was spreading about the miraculous return of the ravens and the restoration of the Tower of London. Police cars and riot vans were arriving. The Eternal Traveller guided Cara away, down onto the muddy river bank.

"There will be chaos awhile yet," she said. "And I think it's time for me to stop travelling, at least for a while. I'll share Grog's soul, perhaps, or one of the other ravens'. I'll keep an eye on things here, make sure it settles down. You can join me if you want."

Cara held her breath. The Eternal Traveller was proposing death, but not as extinction; as change. It was a huge and frightening prospect.

"We could be ravens together, flying high when we wanted, but still at home here, in London. And when we were sure the darkworlds would remain sealed, we could leave the ravens. You could visit your loved ones, leave them a sign that you'd been there and then we could travel around the Earth, around the Universe. Perhaps for ever."

The Eternal Traveller fell silent. Cara had a lot of thinking to do. Amid the wail of the sirens, the memories of her life on this beautiful, terrible planet and all the things that might be awaiting her over the years should she choose to live, against the possibilities should she go with the Eternal Traveller, Cara contemplated the proposal.

It took quite some time to come to a decision.

Widdershins

Part One: The Future in Reverse

The girl, ten years old, but who looked younger, was so tired she thought she would fall but her legs would not let her. They *made* her walk, keeping a brisk pace, and she went round the church on the narrow path once more. She was almost back at her starting point again, wondering if her legs would ever stop, when she saw an old woman standing by the little wall that surrounded the church and graveyard, watching her. Normally she would have wished the woman *good afternoon* but she was too tired and in too much of a hurry, and it was probably not afternoon now anyway.

As she got closer, the old woman stared intently at her, and as she drew level the woman put her hands to her face and cried out, as if the girl was horrible to look at. The girl passed by, her legs moving like pistons and by the time she'd finished another circuit the old woman had gone.

Charlotte Skiddaw, sixty-seven years old, but who looked older, hurried away from the church. The track, sloping gently uphill, led to a lane that went uphill to the centre of the village. Charlotte had been looking forward to being back here, seeing the place for the first time in decades, but the sight of the girl was such that she wanted to be away again. She got to the lane and paused for breath, shielding her face as a brief but fierce hailstorm passed overhead.

Half an hour later she was back in the cottage she'd rented for the week, fighting the temptation to leave without even packing. Seeing the girl had been a terrible shock. She had recognised the child immediately, although it was a face she had not seen for nearly sixty years.

It was herself; Charlotte Skiddaw aged ten.

"Everything is a time machine," her grandfather had said, holding a ring that belonged to his own beloved grandmother, and the sight, the touch of it, brought tears to his eyes. Charlotte had been just a babe and it was many years before she realised the enormity of what he had said; at the age of 38, at a picnic with friends in Buckinghamshire, she had found a flint arrowhead on the ground, skilfully shaped by someone tens of thousands of years before. This connection with the deep past had given her motion sickness, as if she had been momentarily yanked backwards through Time and the truth of her grandfather's words had finally struck her.

The memories made her smile, but the ghost of her past, the small figure walking around the desolate church as if possessed, chilled her to the bone. Hard as she tried, she could not remember being there. And the girl did not look like the happy child she remembered herself being. What had happened? If she wanted to know why she had seen herself in the churchyard, she would have to return and attempt to talk to the girl.

She left the cottage again, intending to head back to the church but found herself going into Barchan village instead, as if there might be an answer there. She passed the tiny railway station and remembered that in the terrace opposite was the home of Miss M, the unforgiving English teacher Charlotte had been glad to leave behind when her family had moved away from the village in the first days of 1957. Generations had passed. Miss M would have moved away or died. No one at the school had known her name. She was Miss M to all of them: children, staff and parents. There was a rumour, shared in whispers, that 'M' stood for *Monster*, but it was never said aloud.

"May I help you?" said a voice beside her, startling Charlotte from her memories and giving her another unsettling blast from her childhood. The voice was Miss M's, of that there was no doubt, but the face was barely recognisable, heavily lined under thick foundation, framed by dyed crow-black hair. The woman was making a poor attempt to defy age.

"Miss M? I was a pupil of yours a very long time ago. I doubt you'll remember me. My name's Charlotte Skiddaw."

The old face cracked into a smile. "Poor Charlotte. I remember you."

Charlotte saw her chance. "I don't suppose you remember just before I left. Did anything *particular* happen in 1956? The summer? I was at the churchyard earlier..."

Miss M's smile waned. "Then you should come in."

She led Charlotte in and went to make tea. Charlotte sat in the dustiest room she had ever seen, on a sofa next to a cat that was, in balance, endlessly washing itself.

Miss M set the tray down. "What did you see at the churchyard?" she asked as she poured the tea, her hands trembling slightly.

Charlotte chose her words carefully and almost

backtracked in the same breath. "I saw a ghost. I think I did, anyway."

Miss M handed her a cup of tea the colour of wood.

"You're lucky you found me. No one else hereabouts will talk about such things. You know what you saw. I've seen it, too. The little girl who circles the church."

"If you've seen her," said Charlotte, taking a deep breath, "then you'll know that she looks like me, down to her school uniform."

Miss M looked up, the sternness of her teaching years returning in full force. "I'm not a fool and neither are you. We both know that child is you."

"Alright, let's say it *is* me," said Charlotte. "I've read that ghosts are traumatic memories replayed in a loop, like a record with a closed groove. I didn't think I believed that, but I can't think of another explanation for seeing myself. But what event could be so powerful to have recorded itself, without me having any memory of it?"

"It's not so much you, dear, as the place. It's *wrong* there. The whole area around the church is just wrong. And I have proof."

Miss M had a photograph. Taken by herself in the mid 1940s, it showed a section of the churchyard, near the lych-gate. A cat, slightly blurred in its black and white stillness, was leaping high in the air.

Except, Miss M said, that it wasn't leaping. She had photographed it *flying* over the tombstones. It had begun at one of the old yew trees, circling it several times and, when photographed, was near the end of its journey.

"I have a box of clippings from the local newspaper. Short articles about strange happenings, wrong happenings here, over the years. No one seems to have linked them except me."

Charlotte put her teacup down. Miss M truly believed what she was saying. Charlotte chose to humour her for now.

"So is the churchyard full of ghosts?"

Miss M grimaced.

"No, my dear, I don't think so. You compounded the problem by doing what you did. I said that part of Barchan village is wrong. You could say it's *widdershins*; the wrong way. And that's how you walked around the church.

"You walked widdershins. And part of you has been stuck there ever since."

It was evening by the time Charlotte left Miss M's house. What she had seen in the churchyard had frightened her, and the afternoon with her former teacher had done nothing to reassure her.

Miss M had stated her belief that Charlotte walking anticlockwise around the church had become entangled with the wrongness of the area. If Charlotte were to walk clockwise around the church nine times, the curse would be lifted. Miss M was all for doing it right away, unnerving Charlotte still further by declaring that *she was no safer in daylight than she was in darkness*, but Charlotte insisted on waiting until morning, and they agreed to meet at the lych-gate at first light.

After a long, restless night where Charlotte regretted waiting, she at last made her way to the church. She approached the lych-gate slowly, reluctant to look, but at the same time unable to do anything but stare at the church.

And there, out of the promise of the dawn,

emerged Charlotte Skiddaw, ten years old, still at school, not yet old enough to suffer dreary employment, a short, unhappy marriage, more dreary employment and, more recently, the stiffness and pains of older age. Charlotte Skiddaw, keeping the church to her left, walking the wrong way around it, part of her trapped there while the rest of her moved on and lived her unfulfilling life.

Perhaps this moment was what she had been waiting for all these years; to rescue that spellbound fragment of her, the piece that had defied all known convention.

Miss M arrived. She had wild flowers in her hair, dried herbs in her pocket "for luck and protection," and was carrying her camera. She gave a small, hand sewn bag of herbs to Charlotte.

"Of course, this may not work," said Miss M. "I'm going by what I've learned about this place, folklore, and educated guesswork. But for all I know it might make things worse."

"I see," said Charlotte. "I'll take the risk. Wish me luck."

She walked through the churchyard and stopped at the path, with the church on her right. The next time she saw young Charlotte, she would walk towards her, pass her, and perhaps by the time she had circled the church the girl would no longer be a prisoner.

Young Charlotte appeared, her pace as fast as it had been the day before and the months and years before that. Miss M raised her camera and began shooting.

Charlotte took a step forward, then another. Then she stopped.

This was a unique situation.

Her childhood self was striding towards her. If Miss M was right, Charlotte was about to send her into oblivion. Was the young Charlotte aware of the enchantment, of the passing of Time? Was she capable of thought, feeling, self-awareness? Or was she nothing but a carbon copy, a blank sheet, separated from all the things that made the adult Charlotte who she was?

Young Charlotte approached and passed her. In a moment of inspiration and wild excitement, Charlotte turned and followed.

She would talk to the girl, walk with the young version of herself.

She had to move quickly to catch up, but was aware that Miss M was looking up from her camera, that Miss M was shouting, "No! No! No!"

And that Miss M still had her finger on the shutter, capturing frame after frame even as the older Charlotte Skiddaw caught up with her younger self and faded away, like a shadow when a cloud covers the sun.

Miss M hurried over to where Charlotte had been. The girl, walking alone, had continued as usual and disappeared around a corner of the church. In desperation Miss M waved her arms around, in case Charlotte, invisible, could be found. She clutched only air.

"Charlotte Skiddaw! Come here at once!" she shouted, as in the glory days of her career. Neither the child nor the adult version of Charlotte appeared.

Miss M, for once blessing the fact that she had a digital rather than a film camera, checked the photos she had just taken. There was an almost continuous stream: young Charlotte approaching older Charlotte,

Charlotte turning, drawing level with her younger self, then disappearing as the girl continued.

"She walked widdershins," muttered Miss M. "Now see what she's done."

She flicked through the pictures again.

There! The last photo had something, next to where Charlotte was just a faded outline. Miss M zoomed in to it and almost dropped her camera in fright.

It was a face, peeping out, no doubt, from wherever Charlotte had gone. An ugly face, sandstone red, twisting to look directly at the camera.

A face that was full of *mischief*.

Part Two: Sunwise

She was in the same place, of that she was sure, and yet she was somewhere utterly different. Gone was the early morning, the churchyard, and the shouts of Miss M. Charlotte was standing in full, dazzling sunshine, on a plateau of smooth rock, dotted in places with hairy looking lichen. A short distance away the rock gave way to moorland and on it stood a huge, circular wall. Charlotte spied an opening and, not knowing what else to do, made for it.

The opening had no door, just a stone lintel above and rough moorland grass below. It seemed an unassuming entrance but as Charlotte crossed the threshold something like an electric current passed through her. Here, inside the wall, the atmosphere was different. Before she had time to analyse it she realised that young Charlotte was here, too, briskly walking around the inside of the wall. When the girl approached, Charlotte began walking and this time she kept pace.

"Hello again," she said. "I thought you were in the churchyard."

"I am," said the girl. "But I'm here as well. Are you in both places, too?"

The possibility had not occurred to Charlotte and she found it shocking. "I don't think so. I think I'm just here." She changed the subject. "Why are you walking? You've been doing it a long time."

"Emma dared me to walk the wrong way around the church nine times to make the Devil appear. I'm on my eighth circle now. It does seem to be taking forever."

Charlotte raked through her memories again. Emma Derwent had been her friend all the time she had lived in Barchan, but they had lost touch shortly before Charlotte had moved away and she had not seen or heard from her again. Emma had been full of tricks, quick to dare or even double-dare. Had Emma known what would happen? Charlotte adopted her most serious tone.

"It's time to stop now, Charlotte. Turn around and go the other way. Then you'll be away from here and back in the churchyard."

"I can't!" the girl cried. "I've tried to stop but my legs won't listen to me."

Charlotte was suddenly certain that the strange stone structure was keeping the girl on her endless walk. She followed her around her circular path and as she passed near the opening she grabbed her and dragged her through. She held her as the girl's legs continued moving, eventually slowing down to a halt.

Exhausted, young Charlotte slept. The exertion had tired both of them and adult Charlotte rested a while before leaving the girl lying on the grass. Having no wish to go inside the structure again, she looked through the entrance once more—noting the two tiers at the top of the wall (which was all the structure appeared to be), worn down by who knew how many feet over numerous years, and the sets of steps leading up to them—before making her way around the outside.

It was impossible to tell the age of the thing. The stone was damaged in places, the steps crumbling, with plants growing from cracks in the mortar, but it was far from ruinous. While she felt sick with anxiety and dearly wanted to return to the churchyard and Miss M, she was desperate to spend a little more time here and question her younger self before finding a way back to the churchyard and walking clockwise around it.

It was only now that Charlotte realised how thin the air was, how she could only breathe in short gasps. She looked away from the structure and saw the peaks of a range of mountains, capped with snow, protruding from the clouds. The plateau, then, was on a mountaintop, with what appeared to be sheer drops on all sides. There had to be a way up here and down again. Otherwise how could the stone structure have been built? The air crackled around her like static electricity, and here and there appeared small orbs of light. They flew awhile and then disappeared.

Charlotte shivered in the chill wind and, concerned for the young girl, was about to return to her when the plateau shook, nearly knocking her off her feet. As she regained her balance, something rose from the sheer mountainside in front of her. At first Charlotte thought it was a small moon but it rotated to reveal a gigantic face, the eyes open and staring, the expression blank. Charlotte's instinct was to run but before she could summon the energy to turn away the huge mouth opened and a thousand screaming creatures ran out to meet her.

Miss M, alone in the churchyard, sat on the coffin rest, wondering what to do. Her scrapbooks, notebooks, and photographs were all at home. There would surely be an answer amongst them, she thought, and went there.

As she opened the front door she heard music coming from the lounge. She knew she had not left the radio on and she crept silently to the door. Inside was the red-skinned figure who she'd photographed in the churchyard. It was holding a wooden box and turning a handle set into it. As the handle moved the music, a dismal fairground drone, played.

The creature was dancing. Dressed in what looked like an oversized cheesecloth shirt and trousers, it stamped around, sucking puffs of dust from the air towards its feet. Its back to the door, Miss M noted with disgust the square cut in the creature's trousers to reveal its buttocks. It danced full circle, the hurdy-gurdy wailing, only stopping when it faced Miss M. The creature's movements were odd, jerky. It was as if the creature had been filmed walking backwards, and was now being played in reverse to give the impression of forward movement.

"A fair swap," it said, its voice gurgling through water that poured from its mouth. "One of you in my world, me in yours."

"But she didn't mean to go. She'll want to come back, just as you'll want to go home, I expect," said Miss M, trying to find her teacher's confidence again.

"All in good time," said her guest. "We can have merriment first." It began to wind the horrible instrument again.

This was too much for Miss M. "Stop that

noise, you... gargoyle!" she cried, addressing it in the only way she could think. After all, with its stony skin, grotesque expression, and dribbling mouth it did resemble one of the gargoyles on the church.

"That's Madame Gargoyle, if you please," said the creature, clearly delighted.

"*Madame Gargoyle*, is it you who's keeping that poor child forever walking in circles?"

Mme Gargoyle stopped winding the hurdy-gurdy. She went, in her strange backwards style, to the window and looked up at the sky.

"I come and go, between here and there. Always such gray skies here, and too much air, enough to make me burst. The child was unlucky, foolish to walk the wrong way in such a place, unlucky because instead of slipping through, as the enchantment should have allowed her to do, she is in two places simultaneously, but at the same time in neither. We know her as The Girl Who Walks. There is nothing I can do, even if I wanted to."

Mme Gargoyle lifted an arm and peered under it at Miss M.

"Your friend is keeping her company now, in one place at least. Forever and ever, I suspect. But never mind them. You have been *watching* for a long time."

A glint of excitement appeared in Miss M's eye. For a moment she forgot the miniature waterfall cascading from Mme Gargoyle's mouth and her odd reverse movements, and began rummaging through her box.

Mme Gargoyle was proof, proof of the wrongness of the area where the church stood.

"This!" she exclaimed, and held up a photograph, dated 7 September 1976, of four orbs of light gathered outside the church. They looked like stars, a constellation.

"And this!" Amongst the photos was a large scale OS map. The village was framed in red pen. The area that included the church, the lane nearby and the houses that stood there were outlined in black. "And these!" More photographs and newspaper clippings appeared.

"Best of all, of course, is you," said Miss M. She grabbed her camera and took a couple of photographs for which Mme Gargoyle posed, giving her most demonic, watery grin. Then Miss M put the camera down.

"Well, now, there are two people down in Hell, or wherever it is you've come from, who don't belong there. What is it going to take to swap places with them? What is it you want?"

"It's not Hell they've gone to! Is that what you thought?" Mme Gargoyle seemed puzzled, offended even. "Hell is here, with its endless rain and its people who have nothing to live for. The Girl Who Walks is happy, even though the enchantment has been only partially successful."

Miss M glared at the creature. "I don't believe you."

"We'll go and ask her, then," said Mme Gargoyle, toying with the hurdy-gurdy's handle. "She can describe the glory of the Sun Palace, where she walks, the honour she has in being part of that sacred place."

Mme Gargoyle, spitting water as her words flooded out, gave praise to all the things that worshipped, and were worshipped, in the Sun Palace. Then they set off for the church. On the way they discussed the orbs in Miss M's photograph.

"Some believe they are the souls of people,

travelling after Death," said Miss M.

"*They* are wrong," said Mme Gargoyle. "Orbs are the souls of *everything* that has lived. People make up but few of them."

Such was the conversation that Miss M was forgetting to be afraid, almost forgetting to be embarrassed at the sight of her companion's bare buttocks. Finally she had found someone who was not afraid to hear that part of the village was not the idyll it appeared to be.

She could almost have felt affection for the slavering Mme Gargoyle had they not reached the churchyard and found no trace of the young Charlotte Skiddaw.

To Charlotte's immense relief, the figures ran past her. She had covered her eyes at first, not wanting to see the details of what she thought was her own death, but as the figures began to lumber around her and away, she dared to look.

Some ran on two legs, some on four or six. One, with an angular head and a mouth that looked like a trumpet, glanced at her but didn't break stride. None were like anything she'd ever seen before, but their excitement at being on the plateau was quite contagious. A quick look behind her made their destination clear; they were heading into the stone structure. Charlotte turned back and came face to face with one of the figures, standing silently a few inches from her. Its face was covered in soft, gray hair, its eyes wide open, looking at her with gentle curiosity. Then it was away, its furry breasts swaying as it went to join its fellows, screaming with excitement.

Young Charlotte was standing by the entrance.

She'd forgotten the girl. Cursing her tardiness,

Charlotte hurried over to her. The girl was happily watching the structure fill with the peculiar creatures, completely unafraid. She seemed happy to see Charlotte.

"You broke the enchantment! Who are you? How did you get here?"

So many questions, Charlotte wasn't sure where to begin.

"You must still be exhausted," she said. "It looks as if I've only broken part of the enchantment; we're both still here. And I don't even know where *here* is."

"It's Fairyland," said the girl. "That's where Emma Derwent said I'd go. I was scared, I thought it was going to be dark and horrible. Has Emma come back yet?"

Charlotte didn't have the heart to tell her the truth; that Emma must have seen something incredibly strange had happened and had left her friend to whatever fate had befallen her.

But then, how many good people of Barchan had seen the two versions of Charlotte? One trapped in the churchyard, the other, oblivious, continuing as normal before moving to another part of the country?

"There's a lot I don't know, Charlotte. But since my name is also Charlotte, I shall call you Lottie. Otherwise we'll all get confused. Now, we have to get away from here and back to Barchan."

"But I like it here. And there's going to be a ceremony in the Sun Palace. Come and see."

Charlotte gave in. After all, she didn't know how to return or even if it was possible.

The Sun Palace had been transformed. Silent, like a monument, when she had first seen it, the creatures had brought the place to life. The charge of energy she'd felt when first crossing the threshold had intensified and every atom of her tingled. The tiers were crowded with agitated figures, the last few clambering up, leaving only Charlotte and Lottie at ground level. Flags and banners hung from the walls. It was as if a circus for the insane was taking place.

And if this was the audience, what in God's name would be the ringmaster?

More mundane things were closer to hand. Charlotte heard a squeal of relief and found Lottie crouched at the wall, knickers around her ankles, splashing water over the rough grass. Charlotte stepped in front of her. If the structure was the religious building she suspected it to be, the assembled crowds could take offence.

But no one took notice of either of them. Evidently something far more important was going to happen. The sun was directly above the centre of the Palace now, its rays turning the stone translucent. Charlotte laid a hand on it. It was warm, with a current like an electrical charge. And it felt fluid. The stone was no longer completely solid.

In fact it felt as if she could fall right through the wall.

She caught a glimpse of a tombstone and thought; *the churchyard!* She was about to reach for Lottie and see if it was possible to just walk through the stone and home again when something brushed past her, coming the other way, and the wall was solid again.

Something had come through and it had brought Miss M with it. It looked like a devil made of sandstone.

Lottie, embarrassed at the sight of the old woman, yanked her knickers back up and stood.

After Charlotte and Miss M had congratulated themselves at finding one another, Mme Gargoyle expressed surprise at seeing Lottie freed from her endless walk. She sprayed the girl with water as she spoke.

"The Girl Who Walks is free! How did you repair the enchantment?"

A little afraid, Charlotte stared at Mme Gargoyle, then saw Miss M smiling and nodding encouragement, so she replied.

"I pulled her through the doorway. That bit was easy. But I'm worried about her. I want to take her home."

"The enchantment will remain for ninety-nine years," said Mme Gargoyle. "Or is it nine hundred and ninety-nine? She cannot leave before that time, so legend has it."

Mme Gargoyle gestured around the Sun Palace. "This is what you have seen and sensed all this time," she said to Miss M. "Time, universes, dimensions, they overlap and cross each others' paths."

The creature with the trumpet mouth appeared from the crowd and pushed its way to a nearby set of steps. It bellowed at them, a series of grunts and growls issuing from the trumpet. Mme Gargoyle looked up at the sun.

"Get up onto the tier. The ceremony is about to begin."

They climbed up and were immediately surrounded. Strange skin and smells pressed against them, animated creatures jostled and bickered on either side. For Mme Gargoyle and Lottie it was nothing new, but the others were frightened. They turned to Mme Gargoyle for reassurance but she, too, became swept up in the frenzied air, winding the hurdy-gurdy's handle as if her life depended on it.

Through the doorway came a figure, with

stag's antlers on its head and part of a bleached skull attached to its face. Whether they were part of a costume or its natural features Charlotte couldn't tell. Here, it seemed, anything was possible.

Except for one thing: when the ceremony began, in all its blazing, copulating glory, Charlotte turned Lottie away. This was one experience the child was not going to have.

Part Three: Over the Moon

Everything is a time machine.

It had occurred to Charlotte, even before Mme Gargoyle had appeared to confirm it, that the 'wrong' part of Barchan could be a time machine, and perhaps it was, but when she grasped Lottie and prevented her from witnessing the ceremony, she realised that the girl was one as well.

Charlotte had never been able to remember taking on Emma Derwent's dare. She barely remembered visiting the church as a child except for Christmas services, but as she held Lottie she felt a lurch of motion sickness and she was back at the churchyard with Emma nearly sixty years before. Emma teased her reluctance to accept the dare, of being afraid of being whisked off to Fairyland, and Charlotte gave in. She walked the wrong way around the church. How many times? Eight. Then she noticed that Emma had gone, so she abandoned the last circuit and sat down for a while before going home.

The part of her that had escaped had been too afraid to complete the dare. The other part remained and would have circled the church, and the inside of the Sun Palace, forever if the older Charlotte Skiddaw had not returned to Barchan.

Charlotte returned to the present and looked down at Lottie, who was giggling and trying to see the ceremony. What else had she witnessed, or even participated in, over the years? Of the two of them, who had lived the worthier life?

After the ceremony had ended, and Mme Gargoyle had insisted on enjoying every visceral moment of it, the four explored the plateau. The huge face with the open mouth still stared out from the mountain's edge and Mme Gargoyle took them to it. Close up, it was clearly made of stone. They ran their hands across the smooth carving, admiring the stonemason's skills.

"We live in the tunnels of the mountains," said Mme Gargoyle, gesturing at the mass of peaks around them. "Drilled by glacial water a million years ago. The head transports us to the plateau and the Sun Palace. Unless we can find other ways up," she said with a glint in her eye.

Miss M crossed herself and shivered in the cold, bright air.

"After what I've just seen, I think I was right about this place first time. It *is* a Hell of sorts, peopled by devils and heathens. I've spent most of my life trying to discover what was wrong in the village and now I wish I hadn't. I want to go home," she said.

"Oh please, Miss," said Lottie. "Can't we spend a little more time in Fairyland? The fairies are such nice people."

Miss M shivered again. "You, dear child, are the innocent caught up in all this. You should not have done what you did but I don't believe you knew what you were getting yourself into. But fairies are *not* nice." She looked at Mme Gargoyle. "I don't think you mean real harm and I found our talk most interesting. Please let us return to Barchan. You may visit whenever you please."

Charlotte grabbed her arm. "Don't you think we should find out more?" she hissed. "How will Lottie *be* if she's back with us? *Can* she be?"

Mme Gargoyle blew water from her mouth, spraying them all, clearing her voice to speak.

"Does The Girl Who Walks *want* to return to the gray skies?"

Lottie looked up at them all. "I want to see Mummy and Daddy."

Charlotte sighed. Her parents had died almost twenty-five years ago, the loss an ever present ache in her chest. She took Lottie's hand.

"Come for a walk with me. I have to tell you something."

Even from a distance, Miss M and Mme Gargoyle could clearly see the moment Lottie began to cry.

In Barchan, things were changing.

The *wrongness* of one part of the village, where universes had overlapped for tens of thousands of years, was becoming more so. The church, deliberately built on a Bronze Age sacred site, which had been deliberately placed on an area known from the Stone Age as magical, began to display visions, both of the dead in its churchyard and of scenes of the plateau and the Sun Palace.

The universes were beginning to separate.

Lottie still wanted to go home. She wanted to see her house, to knock at the door, convinced Charlotte had made a mistake and her parents were still there. Charlotte had not told the girl everything, one incredible fact at a time was enough, and she hid as best she could her fears of what might happen to Lottie if she reappeared in Barchan.

Mme Gargoyle, the hurdy-gurdy now slung around her side, only shrugged. "You must all do as you will. The Girl Who Walks is enchanted and may not be able to leave, or may suffer disastrous consequences if she does leave, but it is her right to try."

She took them along a narrow path around the mountainside, dizzyingly close to the edge. Away from the stone head, out of sight of the Sun Palace, stood a gigantic rock, weathered into a magnificent sculpture, like the tooth of a monstrous cat looming over them. At the back of the rock was a fissure. Mme Gargoyle squeezed into it and the others followed. When they were well inside, enough for the dazzling daylight to be no more than a slit, they reached a junction. Mme Gargoyle pointed a shadowy, jerky hand at it.

"That way descends into the mountain. Not many know it. We go forwards."

Ahead they went, towards what looked like solid rock. Charlotte, at the back of the little group, expected to find the way barred at any moment, but they kept on and suddenly they were in the shade of the yew trees in the churchyard.

And the place was full of people.

Charlotte kept Lottie, who seemed to have suffered no ill effects from the journey, close by. She assumed they had arrived at the end of a wedding or funeral, but when she looked at the people she realised they were separate, unaware of one another, but moving in similar patterns and formations.

They were ghosts.

Miss M gasped; the orbs that she had captured on film, and which flew so freely around the Sun Palace, had taken form.

"Are they dancing?" asked Charlotte.

"Of course they are," said Lottie. "Can't you hear the music?"

There was, indeed, music playing. It was coming from the church. The four made their way around the ethereal figures and Miss M gave the church door the shove it had always needed to open fully.

The church was empty but music echoed around the walls. It was not a hymn or the church organ playing, but something resembling classical music, only twisted, perverse. Miss M crossed herself again and Charlotte was tempted to even though she had no faith. Images of the plateau and the mountain ranges, sometimes a figure from the Sun Palace, flashed though the building like a faulty projection.

Mme Gargoyle clearly recognised the music. She hauled the hurdy-gurdy into position and began to play along then hurried outside. She was greeted by screams, not from the ghosts, who continued their lonely dances, but from the villagers, who could no longer ignore the strange things that went on in Barchan.

Lottie ran out first and joined the dancers. Miss M and Charlotte followed. Miss M grabbed Mme Gargoyle's rough, red arm.

"What's happening? This is like decades of events at once!"

"I don't know," said Mme Gargoyle, padding from side to side. "Perhaps our universes are moving, coming closer together."

"Or could it be they're pulling apart?" cried Miss M.

Mme Gargoyle's eyes widened. "That is possible! Either way, I should return. But first, a little merry-making."

She turned and spat a jet of water into the face of a man who was approaching from behind, fist raised for attack. Miss M recognised him. He had been a neighbour of hers for years. He screamed and clawed at his face as if the water was acid.

Most of the other spectators were frozen in fear, although some turned and ran.

Mme Gargoyle made her way around the graves, the hideous sound of the hurdy-gurdy in full, unrelenting flow. As she passed Charlotte and Miss M, she called to them.

"If our universes are indeed parting, you each have a choice to make. The Girl Who Walks appears to be in good health, but her enchantment may not be broken and she may die if she stays. And what about yourselves? Your neighbours will forever associate you with this blasphemy, this sorcery, this obscenity! Will you stay under the gray skies, or return with me?"

The fracture was increasing. The ghosts stopped dancing and began to turn dizzying, anti-clockwise circles until they broke apart and dispersed like a morning mist. The vision of the Sun Palace came cartwheeling through the church wall, shafts of darkness appearing from the cracks that were breaking the vision apart. Mountains surrounded the village, hemming it in claustrophobically.

Miss M was in no doubt as to what she would do. Fantastic as it was that she had been proved beyond all doubt not to be the old madwoman she was often dismissed as, Barchan was her home. She could no more leave it, especially to join the naked heathens of so-called Fairyland, than fly. To not see Mme Gargoyle again, and discuss how the laws of physics had been bent and broken, was regrettable, but unavoidable.

Lottie, now without dance partners, was standing still. Charlotte put an arm around her.

"Lottie, you can come with me if you like. I live a long way from here, but it's a nice town and not far from the sea."

For whatever time Lottie might have left.

But the girl had her own ideas. "I want to go home. I want to *go back* to Mummy and Daddy."

Charlotte gazed at Mme Gargoyle, still playing the hurdy-gurdy as she made her slow, jerky way back to the yew trees and her route home. Was it possible for Lottie to return to 1956, even for a moment? And if so, could Charlotte go with her and see her parents once more?

Charlotte hurried to catch up with Mme Gargoyle.

"I think we've all chosen the gray skies."

Mme Gargoyle raised a red eyebrow.

"Lottie thinks she can go back in time and see her parents," Charlotte continued. "*Our* parents."

Mme Gargoyle considered it. "She has a foot in two worlds, neither of which is the here and now."

She let the hurdy-gurdy's handle go. The instrument's drone faded away. "She is of the past. You are not. You must go forward, either here or with me. What is here for you? In my home you'll find elation, despair, joy and desolation, all with the creatures you consider so abhorrent."

And for one ludicrous moment Charlotte was tempted to go.

The yew trees always provided shade, or shelter, but one patch of shade was darker than the rest. It formed a neat, narrow slit that could not be accessed by accident. Mme Gargoyle was looking through, mindful of the increasing void, when Lottie came to say goodbye. She gave the strange, red figure a hug.

"You carry the past with you," said Mme Gargoyle. "Capture it if you can. A moment may last forever if you are fortunate. But if you are not, you will not be able to return to the Sun Palace."

"I'll miss you and the other fairies."

"We will miss The Girl Who Walks," said Mme Gargoyle.

Lottie approached Charlotte and Miss M. The last of the villagers was walking away, after one last glare at the two women.

"I wonder if they will tolerate me now," said Miss M. She focussed on Charlotte. "I suppose you'll go home. You can leave all this behind."

"I'm not sure I want to," said Charlotte. "Lottie believes she can see her parents again. I'd dearly like to go with her, but it would be wrong, even harmful, for them to see me."

Seeing Miss M's quizzical expression, Charlotte explained, as best she could, how her grandfather's statement may have been more than a mysterious comment.

Miss M was incredulous. "*The child* is a Time Machine? You can't let her believe such nonsense. Her house has a young family living in it. Lottie will have her heart broken if she goes there. What then?"

"I believe she won't. Mme Gargoyle thinks it's possible that Lottie takes a piece of her own Time with her. Even if it's just for a moment, she will be happy. Wouldn't *you* like to see your parents again?"

Miss M wrinkled her face. Charlotte took a deep breath and continued.

"What about going with Mme Gargoyle? I

admit it's crossed my mind to."

"Are you insane?" Miss M nearly shrieked. "What we have found is fantastic beyond anything I've imagined was happening all these years. But it is a depraved place, full of savages. If these two places are pulling apart, then so be it. Barchan will be what it always should have been."

"No more flying cats in the churchyard? No more streets and houses where things don't happen as they should? What about your life's work?"

"I never asked for it. I shall be glad it's over. Did you see those people? My neighbours? They were angry and frightened, but they were not surprised. No one ever talked about these things, but they were whispering about them, you mark my words."

Lottie was reaching for Charlotte's hand and shrinking a little from Miss M. At that moment Charlotte made up her mind.

"They're not savages, Miss M," she said. "They're just...*widdershins*. They looked after a child for nearly sixty years. The creatures that came out of that stone mouth are very strange but that doesn't make them dangerous. What more can I do here? We've rescued a part of me that was trapped. *I* feel freer now. If Lottie has it in her to see our parents again then I can do something that's difficult and frightening, too. I'm going with Mme Gargoyle."

Lottie was delighted. Miss M gaped, then set her face as it had been for much of her life, erring on the side of displeasure. She did, however, concede something, be it curiosity, jealousy or admiration, Charlotte couldn't tell, by taking her camera from her bag and handing it to her.

"It does still photography and video recording. You might want to document what you find. In case you're ever able to return."

They both knew that it was hardly likely; the two universes had lived together for who knew how long. Moving apart would be an event of monumental importance, something that could only happen once in the blink of an eye that was their lifetimes. But it was something for Charlotte to hold on to from home and contained photos of the village, Miss M's cat, even a self-portrait: Miss M, unsmiling, at arm's length.

Charlotte still felt unhappy about letting Lottie go home alone, but Lottie insisted that only babies were accompanied for such a short distance. Charlotte remembered the way, across the field next to the church, down to the end of a short lane. It was quiet, safe. She hoped with all her heart that Lottie found what she needed there.

Mme Gargoyle was beckoning, the water from her mouth pooling around her feet.

"Good luck, Miss M," said Charlotte. "Thank you for everything. Without you I think I would have gone mad. I would certainly never have got this far. Will you be alright?"

"I expect I shall be fine," said Miss M. "The rocking of boats is not often done in Barchan. Everyone will forget. They'll make sure of it."

Mme Gargoyle disappeared into the void in the shade of the yew trees, with Charlotte close behind.

Miss M looked around. She was alone. The mountains that surrounded Barchan were fading. She wondered how long it would be before all traces of Barchan's otherness disappeared, how Lottie and Charlotte would fare. Poor Charlotte; she had always felt sorry for the girl and she did now for the woman, although she couldn't say why.

She walked home, refusing to acknowledge

the shower of rain that soaked her and the stares of some of those who had witnessed the visions in the churchyard. As soon as the rain had passed over, Miss M hauled the brazier to the middle of the back yard. She began a fire, using old newspapers and kindling. When she was sure the fire had taken hold, she went indoors, happy to see her cat, Louis, had settled down after thoroughly sniffing everywhere Mme Gargoyle had trodden.

The boxes, with every photograph and every newspaper clipping she had ever collected about the village, and all the bundles of papers she had typed out over several decades, sat in the lounge. She picked them up, took them to the back yard and there she stood, watching the flames, casting the papers into them, one by one, until long after sunset.

After Wor(l)ds

My mother's side of the family has long been cursed with horrific nightmares and I've spent my 47 years on this planet continuing that tradition. They are brutal, monstrous and terrifying to the point where I wake up paralysed by fear. But the other dreams I have act as a balance, a blessing: outrageous structures, super-real landscapes, familiar planets glowing with unfamiliar colours, birds in phenomenal numbers. I wake from these dreams exhausted, and why not? I have, after all, just been a long way from home.

I grew up in an ordinary looking terraced house on the outskirts of London. No Gothic mansion this, but it was as haunted as you'll find in any classic ghost story. It was a restless spirit who I assumed at the time was malevolent but who knows? It may not have been aware of how frightening it was: I'd lay awake when everyone was asleep, listening to *someone* climbing the stairs. One night I watched as my bedroom door opened and a silhouetted figure walked towards my bed. When it reached out and gripped the bedstead I screamed and it dissolved. I sometimes heard whispered conversation outside my (first storey) window. On one occasion footsteps made their noisy way downstairs, the door handle to the hall turned and then – nothing. On opening the door there was no one there, much to the relief of my brother, sister and I. I dreamt about the house for years after we moved out, the ghost screaming with rage as I was forced to walk towards the door. Have I ever been back there in the three decades since I left? Of course not!

Along with the occult, music has been my lifelong obsession. Once I'd realised that I needed to write horror stories (in the early 1990s), I found that certain pieces of music radically changed my frame of mind. This is what many musicians seek to do, of course, but I found that two albums in particular – 'The Monstrous Soul' by Lustmord and 'Horse Rotorvator' by Coil – played repeatedly inspired all kinds of visions and put me in the right place to channel them and everything I was dreaming about into a coherent and, hopefully, constructive form.

I still use these techniques – I do write in silence at times, but the 'right' music is infinitely preferable. It's a matter of continually trying to push my imagination to its limit but also to explore my conviction that there are things outside and beyond the world that we see around us. I've had many experiences that I can't rationally explain and I want to reach out to what's beyond our everyday existence. At the same time, I've always been painfully aware of politics, social injustice, the horrors that people inflict on one another. To ignore these issues is, to me, unforgivable.

To still describe what I write as 'horror' is somewhat inaccurate. I've changed over the last twenty-five years, so my writing has, too. The term 'slipstream' is probably where I feel closest to home – crossing boundaries, in life as well as in genres of writing, is what I have always tried to do. The stories contained in this issue of Storylandia have far more of a spiritual consciousness to them than my early work.

Moving from London to West Cornwall – the far west of England, still known for its witches, stone circles and ancient burial chambers – has inevitably altered my view of the world. But don't expect a conventional happy ending or even a definite ending at all: I don't believe stories really have an end, rather a point where we have to leave them. A storyteller's job is to show the reader certain episodes from another world or place. It can only be a fleeting glimpse, because where exactly do things end? In death?

Are you sure?

Julie Travis
West Cornwall, November 2014

www.julietravis.wordpress.com

Julie Travis has been writing horror and dark fantasy fiction since the early 1990s, after a youth spent watching horror films, writing music fanzines and playing bass guitar in a punk band. Her short stories and novellas, which have been compared to Clive Barker, Thomas Ligotti, Catherynne M. Valente and the Stephen King/Peter Straub collaborations, have been published widely in the British and North American slipstream/horror small press, including REM, Kimota, The Third Alternative (now known as Black Static), Psychotrope, Saccade, Premonitions: Causes For Alarm (which received an Honourable Mention in Ellen Datlow's Year's Best Horror 2009), Covers of Darkness, Aphelion, Kzine, Urban Occult and two previous issues of Storylandia. She has also appeared in two queer anthologies: Necrologue - the Diva Book of the Dead and the Undead (nominated for the Gaylactic Spectrum Literary Award 2004) and Va Va Voom, has written numerous articles for the gay press and co-founded the Queeruption international music and politics festival. Born in London in 1967, she now lives by the sea in West Cornwall and spends much of her time at stone circles and other sacred sites.

www.ingramcontent.com/pod-product-compliance
Lightning Source LLC
Chambersburg PA
CBHW070939130626
46555CB00001B/500